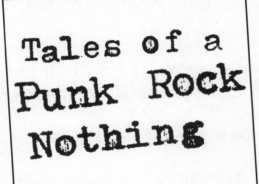

Tales of a Punk Rock Nothing

by
Abram Shalom Himelstein
and
Jamie Schweser

This book is a work of fiction. All names, characters, places, and incidents are the products of the authors' feeble imaginations, or are used fictitiously. Any resemblance to actual persons, living or dead, events or locales is entirely coincidental. They were trying to write a story about a wandering barbarian in the middle ages, but it didn't work out.

Published by New Mouth from the Dirty South

Copyright Abram Shalom Himelstein and Jamie Schweser 1998, 2000. All rights reserved.

Cover photo by Carl Schweser

This is the third edition. Too bad you weren't cool enough to get a copy of the first or second. They're gonna be worth a dollar or two in a thousand years or so. Don't worry though, everything in this edition is the same. (Except for the previous sentence, and this one, too.)

Copies of this book are $10 postpaid in the United States. More elsewhere.

New Mouth from the Dirty South
PO Box 19742
New Orleans LA 70179-0742

Send us your letters. We write back. Eventually.

books@newmouthfromthedirtysouth.com

www.newmouthfromthedirtysouth.com

ISBN 0-9666469-0-8

*This book is dedicated to good parents,
especially ours.*

"Every fury on earth has been absorbed in time, as art, or as religion, or as authority in one form or another. The deadliest blow the enemy of the human soul can strike is to do fury honor. Swift, Blake, Beethoven, Christ, Joyce, Kafka, name me a one who has not been thus castrated. Official acceptance is the one unmistakable symptom that salvation is beaten again, and is the one surest sign of fatal misunderstanding, and is the kiss of Judas."

James Agee in *Let Us Now Praise Famous Men*

Editor's Note

I came into possession of these documents as Elliot's half of the Hannah Rosenberg Doesn't Run Away in 1995 Treaty. When I decided to make a book out of this, Elliot was reluctant, but eventually went for the I-need-some-kind-of-project-to-keep-my-sanity-intact excuse.

I promised Elliot that he wouldn't have to deal with the sorting through, editing, or publishing of this, and he has made me honor my word. Repeated requests for a bit of extra information to round out the story have only elicited muttered responses such as: "Jonah... Nineveh..." and, "You are your own whale."

I'd like to thank Maureen for letting me use letters by her and to her, and for her time and help.

I've kept editing down to a minimum. I've fought off the urge to underline sections and add some study questions. Documents are placed in my closest reconstruction of chronological history. The only major changes are that the journals and letters, which were originally hand-written, have been typed and titled.

The story might be tidier with a suicide, or a drug overdose, or a graffiti-covered tombstone in Paris. What actually happened isn't nearly as profitable for the record company, but more pleasant for his family. I know there are things in here that make Elliot cringe, but the whale has carried me to this shore, and I have only these pages to offer.

My first editorial effort. Dig in. It tastes better than it looks.

Sincerely,
Hannah Elise Rosenberg, literary executor

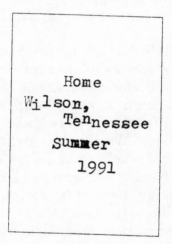

Home
Wilson,
        Tennessee
Summer
     1991

June 9, 1991

Dear Maureen,

So not only did you leave me alone in this hell-hole, it's actually gotten more hellish, if that's possible. More ugly, more pathetic and twisted. But I'm sure the bird has sung long distance by now. Her worst expectations confirmed. But to tell the truth, I'd really like to write about something else first. Not that I have any good news, I'm just sick of dealing with the worst news, so I'll start with the mediocre.

A party at Andy Davis's house, just like the hundreds of others parties of that nature, so I guess I should spare you the details, but then this letter would be less than a page long, and since I'm expecting more from you, here goes:

The usual. Beer. Meatheads. Airheads. I'm talking to Teeters in a field at the edge of the noise of Deathhorse's hard rock covers. He's telling me about his year in Knoxville and wonders if I'm going. And I'm still not. More time with the Teeterses of the world? Um, fuck you, but no.

Then the inevitable. Ooh, a fight. Like iron shavings toward a magnet, like Ma ringing the dinner bell; all the children come running. (I'm pretty sure that if you walked into a city council meeting and yelled "Fight!" you could clear the room as everyone would leave to watch.) I made it to the keg just in time to see Jason going at it with The Steroid King. Seems they'd had a disagreement over the existential meanderings of Camus versus Sartre, and how it related to who was next in the keg line. S.K. convinced J of Sartre's superior intellect and Colin and I got to carry Jay to the station wagon.

We drove out to Wal-Mart to wait for Jay to sober up so we wouldn't have to carry him into his house.

We were a little representational painting of America right there: teenage boys in a Ford, 1/3 drunk and recently involved in a brawl. Where's Norman Cockwell when you need him?

That's when the cops arrived to put us in our place/ save the Wal-Mart parking lot from us ruffians. Officer Richard Plummer remains his usual genius self.

On the way to Jay's house, we were at the red light on Highway 47 when this Rolls Royce pulled up next to us. (Rich guy dialogue: "Hey let's go do some lines of coke in Wilson." ????) Jay sits up looking Raging Bull. He started rolling down the window. (I'm thinking about staying up an extra two hours, washing the car so his vomit doesn't ruin the paint job, airing it out, making sure that my parents don't smell Jay and ask questions. Thinking about what geniuses my friends are, and what a genius I must be for being their friend.)

Jay started screaming out the window, in an ultra-country voice, "Hey, is that a Rolls Royce?!?" He got no response, so he opened the door and stumbled out into the street, and, much to the rich fucker's horror, started tapping on the window. "Hey, I seen one just like that on *Lifestyles of the Rich and Famous*! Hey, are y'all famous? Hey look at that boys, it's a real live Rolls Royce." Since my choices for friends seem to be drunken idiots or drunken idiots, I'm glad that I picked the funny drunken idiot.

Then, on Thursday, as if this town isn't already enough of a pile of shit, I managed to add my name to the anus of its history. When the shit hits the fan, it really splatters, and in this case it was a lot of shit, and I'm sure it's splattered pretty far. I thought maybe I could write a letter fast enough for you to get it and use it as some sort of turd umbrella or something, but I didn't send it in time. Anyway, I'm sure you've already heard about my adventures in glass work, seeing as how news travels faster than it happens. (Not that I would ever say that certain people around here gossip too much, no I would never say that.) Letter enclosed, nuff said.

Sorry this is so short. I'll write another letter that's more flowery and nice when I'm feeling less suicidal.

-Elliot

June 26, 1991

Dear Mr. Easterling,

This is a hard letter to begin, but I'll start with what I want to be the theme for this letter: I am sorry and embarrassed for what I did to your store. There are no excuses for what I did, but I'm going to try to explain why I did it.

What I did was wrong. It made things worse. I hope that this letter does the opposite. I hope you'll read this.

On Thursday I stopped by your store to pick up a sprinkler for my dad. I walked in and waved to Paul Nicholson and found the sprinkler. As I approached the counter, you were talking on the phone, and I heard you say, "Bout the only thing that you can trust a nigger to do is to steal." You looked up and saw me there, sprinkler in hand. I almost swiveled my head to exchange glances with Paul, to let him know that I didn't share your racist opinion. But he already knows how you feel, and I didn't want to drag him into any disagreement with his employer.

I think you knew that I didn't share your feelings, but you lowered the phone and smiled, "Well, it's

4

the truth ain't it?" I should have walked out. But you told me a price, and I handed you some money, and then you gave me my change like nothing had happened.

At home I sat in my room and replayed again and again what you said. And how I didn't look at Paul. And wondered if Paul thought that I was a racist for not saying anything back to you. I worried that Paul might think that me being a racist was the reason that we weren't friends after sixth grade. Paul and I had been friends all through grammar school. But then we got to middle school, and we haven't spoken much since. And I worried that Paul thinks that it's because I don't like black people, or I think that black people "can't be trusted."

I started to get angry, thinking about how crappy the whole thing was, remembering all the foul, rotten parts of Wilson. Things I usually try not to remember. Like how mad I was when my mom wouldn't let me have a study date with Nileen Morehead because, "People might get the wrong idea and burn the house down." Or the time my father and I drove to Covington to get new tags for the car and were "greeted" by a gang of KKK in full robe. When one of them forced literature through my open, passenger-side window, that was the first time that I had seen fear on my father's face.

That night, at dinner, I told my parents about what happened, and they said that we wouldn't shop at your store anymore, but somehow that just didn't seem like any consolation. It didn't square things up.

I was lying in bed, and I couldn't sleep. I kept hearing what you said, and getting madder and madder at you and more and more embarrassed. Finally I just couldn't take it anymore, grabbed my baseball bat, went to your store and broke the windows. I mean all of this not to excuse what I did, but to begin to explain.

There's this part of Judaism that goes like this: God created the world imperfect, with flaws, and then created humans to straighten out the problems. It's called Tikkun Olam, which means "Fixing the World." There are a lot of things about my religion that have been difficult to understand and follow, but the idea that this world is messed up seems pretty true, and I accept that it's all of our of jobs to make the world better. Which I didn't do when I broke your windows with a baseball bat. Which I am trying to do now with this letter.

In closing, I'd like to tell you what I wish that I had done. When you said that stuff about black people, I should have said, "I don't agree," put down my purchase on the counter and walked out. I wouldn't have had to look at Paul to show him that I was on his side.

At the dinner table (before I broke your windows) my mother said that I should write you a letter explaining how I felt, and I thought that it wasn't enough. And here I am, with the beginnings of a criminal record, four hundred dollars for the poorer, writing the letter I should have written that night.

I hope this letter, in some way, starts to make things better.

Sincerely,
Elliot Rosenberg

July 8, 1991

Maureen-

A jail break has been planned. I wanted to wait for your conjugal visit, but a month and a half feels like a forever right now. It couldn't stay this shitty-

well maybe it can stay this shitty - but I'm leaving.
DC bound. Not Knoxville. Not college. Not Wilson til I die. Deeee Seeee, you see.

This is the story: me and Colin went to see Marchenko play in Memphis. Since I went with Colin, we left late, and when we got there this band, Three On The Tree, were already playing. It was the antithesis of a big rock show. It was at this warehouse by the river. No stage, no extra lights, no backstage, the bands were hanging out and talking to people in the audience. Plus no one was drunk. Plus it only cost five bucks, and it wasn't in a bar or anything, these guys just rented the warehouse and had the show there. Two other bands played before Marchenko, and then when Marchenko played, it was totally packed and people were going ape-shit, and there was this big circle of people slamming in front. The band stopped the show and asked people to settle down so everyone could have fun and not get hurt. They also talked about a lot of their songs before they played them. One was about this big police brutality thing in DC. Every song built up into swirling madness until it seemed like all the equipment was broken, and then the next song would start on a dime and do it all over again. They were totally out of control, and played completely tight at the same time. Fucking incredible. Best show ever.

After the show I wanted to ask them questions about DC. They were all drenched in sweat, I was all drenched in sweat. I felt like a geeky groupie or something, but they were really friendly. Ed, the bassist, gave me the number of this house in Arlington (a suburb of DC) called the Positive Change House, which is where he lives with a bunch of other punk people. He said it's a good place to check for rooms in the DC area, since a lot of people move in and out.

So that was it. I was like, "Fuck Wilson, I'm moving to DC." By the time I got home, I could see the Washington Monument on the horizon. I was pretty stoked, but you know, whatever, anywhere would be better than Wilson.

So I called today and talked to a guy there, and it turns out they've got a room opening for two months, starting August 1. The house rules seem cool: no meat, no alcohol, no drugs. It doesn't seem like they have a "You're Going To Hell If You Touch The Stuff" attitude or anything, though.

Tonight I tell my folks. It's been tense around the house since The Incident. They're still less than thrilled about the no-college-right-away decision. But even if college is "really different from high school," I'm in no mood. So things will be easier on everyone if I at least leave town. Even if it's not for Harvard. At least Hannah has been at camp and hasn't had to deal with all of this shit.

Late

Big blow-out with the folks. Done some screaming, some crying. No college = failing at life. Failing 101, enrollment deadline is next week. Here's my deposit, sign me the fuck up. I'm gonna ace this one. Think maybe I'll go out and break some windows. Oh wait, I guess I already passed that class.

4:20 am

Fuck. I can't believe I'm making plans that mean that we won't see each other for a long time. Salivating for a few weeks with you. It's been a long month with no definite plan for escape. And now I have one. I wish that we were running away together, but you've got your escape pod ready, and there's no room, and now I've got one too. I know that you know...

Strange that I know that I'm leaving and you

8

don't know. Strange to make this decision without hearing anything about what you think about any of this. The only good thing here is thinking about how you used to be here. So I should go where there's something better, right? A phone date? I'd really like to hear your voice, and not have a six day lag in communication.

Love,
Elliot

July 20, 1991

Dear Maureen,

Just counting down the days. Going to work. Playing guitar. Now that I'm leaving, I have this urge to find every person in town and tell them exactly what annoys me about them. Today I wrote a song for Missy Johnson.

Big red chewing gum breath, carmex covered
 lips, I want you.
I love the way your hair stands up, up against
 gravity, in open defiance of all that this
 world stands for.
Please teach me the right color blush for the
 natural look.
Please teach me that look, that look that fools
 so many - the dumb, the pseudo-deep, that
 look that makes idiots believe that you
 don't understand the darkness/evilness of
 all that surrounds you.
What inner-strength you show with that fluo-
 rescent green skiing jacket.
Higher you reach, your hair says it all.

Glad to hear that camp is cool. Sounds like you had a good time on your weekend off. It's cool that you've made friends with that German guy. What did he think of the amusement park? Do y'all speak German or English when you're not around the kids?

No word yet from Easterling. It was pretty bizarre, writing that letter as "Elliot the Jew." I forget that lots of people in town think about my family as the Jew Family. Until I'm reminded. Not that I'm not psyched about being a Heeb, but there are some crappy parts, too. Example: there's a prayer that men are supposed to say every day that goes like this, "Thank you, O lord, my god, who did not make me a woman." It ain't all apples and honey, this Jewish Heritage.

In addition to my daily prayers, I've been mixing a new tape for you. And as a special bonus, Rabbi Rosenberg has written some commentary about what the musicians are trying to tell us.

"Dressed to Kill," is on Marchenko's new album. I was lying on my bed a couple nights ago, listening to this, and it hit me that a lot of these songs are about the Gulf War, "Drop one down the chimney/ that's so erotic/ A free vacation/ somewhere exotic" and I was back in the minute when we drove down to Austin so you could check out the school and so I could take a trip with you (and so that we could burn a lot of gas and give America a reason to fight a war for oil). I remembered the "Support the Troops" parade organized by the fraternities, and standing alongside the main street, watching rich frat boys on floats showing their support. Alternately being overwhelmed by how frustrated and small and crushed we were by the whole big war machine, and then rallying again to make sarcastic comments about the parade. My near insane, off key screamed version of "Proud to be an American." And that woman, wearing the "woman:

man = fish: bicycle" t-shirt screaming at the parade over and over, "You fucking idiots. You fucking idiots."

And sleeping with you that night: super fragile creatures clinging and clutching for warmth and comfort in the face of something big and scary and undefeatable.

The thing about mix tapes, and the way that they're like relationships, is that I get to put all the genuinely pretty/interesting parts at the beginning, on the surface, to draw you in, to get you to want to be closer. And once I have you interested, attracted, wanting to know all of me, I show you the more human sides, the less pretty and the more petty. And then I feel cooler and better and more loved because you see all (whatever that means) of me and still love and like and are attracted to me. I try to explain the interesting things that I'm thinking and then hope that you'll still want me even when you know all the depressing shit that comprises large portions of my brain. Some good poetry about some bitter shit. A cut off the new Marchenko album, then here comes a crusty Dylan song.

The next song, "Masters of War," is a, um, folk song, but super important. This is the song that Bob Dylan played on Saturday Night Live the weekend the war started. Of course he was so drunk, or something, that you couldn't understand a word he was singing and it kind of sounded like he was gargling, actually. But I just kept thinking of all the people around our parents' age who used to listen to this stuff and actually believe in it, thinking of them seeing it on SNL and remembering how they used to feel about this song and what it used to mean to them and thinking about what soulless yuppies they've all become. Meanwhile the world has gotten worse, and George Bush got elected, and we were about to start bombing the hell out of another little country far away for our economic interests. Thinking about all those people who saw that and were maybe touched just a little bit, maybe.

Iggy Pop's "I Wanna Be Your Dog." I mean sometimes...

And some Phil Ochs crawled out of my parents record bin."Love Me I'm a Liberal." "Ten degrees to the left of center in good times/ Ten degrees to the right of center when it affects them personally." I used to sit in my room and listen to Phil Ochs and come out and ask my parents to explain all the references in his songs. And then they told me that he killed himself and I haven't listened much lately, but this one song wanted to go here.

"It's Tricky" by Run DMC- I just hope that every time you listen to this tape you'll hear this song and know that I can rhyme your ass into the ground, and wherever you are, however many years from now, you better be ready to do battle.

Soul Side's "Clifton Wall." It's funny that we were almost too shy to go up and talk to them after they played that night, and now I'm going to be living in a house with Ed from Marchenko.

Too much talk.

I like your new way of saying, "I was laughin'."

L-word,

Elliot

Positive
Change
House

Arlington,
    Virginia

    Fall 1991-

  Spring 1992

Tired, but want to write, to record a little. Don't want this to be another failed journal that turns into my math notebook. At least it won't be a math notebook soon. I guess a journal's like flossing. Have to make it a habit, so I just do it every night, like my prayers down on bended knee.

Today I moved out of Wilson. Mom was crying, Dad was flustered. Normal. Hannah cracked funny jokes. Also normal. I got in a car with Colin and Jay. Apples on the tree were ripening and I was glad that I wouldn't be there to rake up the rotten ones.

Positive Change: a house full of punk rockers, but totally suburban looking. No graffiti, you can't tell from the outside. Colin and Jay and I got here at 11:30 and Mike was grumpy about us arriving so late. I guess we should have called. We moved the stuff into my room, and then walked to the 7/11 at the corner. I kept waiting for things to start, for me to meet people and have a job, but everyone was asleep and Colin and Jay just wanted to go to sleep. And I should be sleeping, but I can't, wondering how it's going to be. And hoping that Colin and Jay don't hang out too long, cause I want to look around and meet people alone.

Went out to Taco Bell with Adda, Sean, Jordana. Jordana didn't eat anything. What am I supposed to write? I need a job. Already worried about money, which sucks. There are six 7/11s within walking distance from our house.

Weird to live in a family house with a family of people I don't know yet. Cooking dinner, paying rent, not in my parents' house. This is me, not in college, everyone, especially me, surprised to see me with such an unmapped future. No college-dorm-housemom-cafeteria-meal-plan.

Dear Diary,

Got a job at Dupont Natural Foods. Saturday Adda and Sean gave me a tour of the city. We took the Metro to Dupont Circle in DC. Mass transit is awesome. Supposedly the trains here are so clean that they've been used in movies as scenes where people go to heaven. Stopped by Dupont Foods where Sean works, filled out an application, got called, start in a week. Glad I don't have to flip burgers or something. It should be a pretty cool job. Also cool that I still have a week off. Time to relax, get situated, explore the city.

Atomic Records in Georgetown. Awesome.

Eros Auto Association 7". Kicks ass. Saw first picture of Tina on the back of her record. Now I know what the regular dweller of this room looks like. I found out from a record cover. Fucking weird.

Can't wait to tape Adda's records.

Carnival Plague plays on Thursday. With other bands that Sean and Adda say are really good.

Wish I was at home for Maureen's send off.

Sat around the house and listened to records. I think I'm looking forward of going to work. Tried to call Maureen but it was busy, probably good, it will be cheaper to call later anyway. Think I'll go swing in the park.

Me, Adda, Sean, Ed, Christa and Marian made a big spaghetti dinner and went to the show. El Pollo Negro: big times three, half the smoke of Smiley's, lots of people listening to rock music, Jane's Addiction on the sound system in between bands, I only know five people, but at least I like everyone I know.

Big mast statues over the bar, walls are purple, floor: huge and checkerboard. Little spotlights everywhere that cut through the smoke and illuminate spots on the checkerboard when it's empty and the heads of the crowd when it's full of people.

Even though it's a bar, anyone can get in.

Animal Farm was awesome. They were all wearing paper mache pig heads and fishnet stockings. The slam pit was friendly, swirling bodies, other people in big animal heads who got subjugated and beaten by the band, and a big banner that said "Some Animals Are More Equal Than Others."

Carnival Plague: Spazzy singer looking inbred and dressed up like an 80's new-waver. Hippie bassist, metal guitars, woman drummer who pounded the shit out of it. Rad. Adda said Tim, the singer, is Tina's boyfriend. "Sometimes."

By the end of the show I could have wrung half a cup of sweat out of my shirt.

Stayed up talking with Jordana at home. She's so cool and foxy. Do housemates?

———

And this is me writing in a journal, a parting gift from my parents (with one hundred dollars inside). Which brings me to the question: Why am I writing this? Who's going to read it? Older me? Someone I trust who's rummaging through my personal stuff? Grandchildren? Stealer of a backpack examining the goods?

Whatever. Whoever you are, hopefully you'll see something that doesn't suck.

———

Jordana and Sean and me did Food Not Bombs.

Went around and got expired stuff from all the health food places (and Aaron robin hooded some good stuff from Dupont Nat. Foods). Mike and us three and Liz, Jason, and Nicole all made a big Soup with the vegetables, and sandwiches with the bread and ate health-food donuts while we cooked.

Handed everything out in Lafayette Park. Vegetarian food for free, homeless people and punks and hippies all came. Jordana and Sean are in charge of doing this every Saturday.

Food to the people. Thinking a lot about how much food gets thrown out around me every day. And all day at work I'm surrounded by food. "There's starving children in..." But 40,000 die everyday. Like destroying food to end the great depression. So that "everyone" can eat again. Except the people who forever almost starve until they actually do.

Michael came in today after the lunch rush, he was bossing everyone around:

"Elliot, could you straighten up the soda case? Everyone, while I have your attention, I just want to remind you that you can have one soda on your break, but you have to pay for juice or anything else."

Sean was all smiles and zeal, and went to work. "No problem, Michael! I'm gonna clean up the snack department, okay?" Susan was at the counter looking annoyed, and then Michael took her into the back to talk to her about something, "Elliot, could you take a break from the soda case and watch the counter for a second?"

"No problem, Michael." Maybe I could just run around and get nothing done all day. Sean started acting like he was dancing in a musical, straightening up the snack displays. He was exaggerating all of his movements and making a big production of sticking one of each snack into his jeans pockets.

Then Michael and Susan came out of the back-room, and Sean kept vigorously tidying up the shelves, and shot Michael a big smile. Michael looked all proud and then he left. It turns out he was telling Susan that she needs to "seem happier in the store, especially around the customers."

Sean brought home lots of vegan chocolate bars for everyone. I wonder if Susan will get fired, it seems like she could get on Michael's good side pretty easily, if she just tried a little. It sucks that Sean is Mr. Employee-of-the-Month while he steals lots of shit. But Michael sucks harder.

Tired, but I want to write before I sleep, while it's fresh. Jordana told me tonight that she was molested when she was six/seven. I had no idea what to say. "That really sucks," or "I'm so sorry." All responses sounded wrong in my head. I stayed silent for a while, then asked her how much she thought about it. She said that she thought about it a lot when she first remembered it, but that now she only thinks about it when things remind her, like I had by telling the story of my first grade girl-friend. And for a second I felt shitty about bringing up first grade, but then she seemed just kind of regular, and not upset. Then we played the spitting game, and I got nailed on the eyebrow by her first (and obviously juiciest) lugie.

Back at the house, and the image of some hairy-backed cretin touching a young Jordana has me creeped-out. But it probably wasn't some hairy-back, it was probably someone at church or school or uncle or baby-sitter. And then I think about

Maureen, and visualize her uncle doing that shit to her. And I worry about Hannah, and wonder which is the asshole that might try and pull fucked-up shit with her. And I wonder if the assholes don't have sisters or don't think about them as being like their sisters. But then that's fucked up, because if every girl is like your sister then which ones are you supposed to want to get it on with?

The images of Jordana and Maureen and Hannah won't let me get to sleep, and the usual sleeping pill of masturbation is way out of the question.

That riot grrrl zine makes me think that it's worse than one in four.

On the Metro today, something like this:

Sean: Sucks that Michael is such a dick to Susan.

Me: It seems like if she'd just try to be a little more enthusiastic when he's around that he'd lay off her...

Sean: No way, he just gets off on having the power to tell people how to behave. Besides, why should she be enthusiastic?

Me: Because people don't want to come into a store where everyone is in a bad mood, and Michael wants people to enjoy shopping there, and since he's the boss, we should act friendly so that he'll be happy...

Sean: Whatever, just cause he's the boss doesn't mean he's better than us or something. This job is totally without purpose, other than to make money for his lazy ass. If you're not going to enforce "profit-sharing" by giving

yourself big "discounts," you might
as well scare away all the obnoxious
customers. Lower profits discourage
other people from wasting their lives
on such useless endeavors.

The rest of the way home I felt like such a kiss-
ass. The kid that wants to please the teacher, angry
that the other kids aren't acting quiet enough to
earn the piece of candy for the class. Super lame.
Wilson sucked, but at least I got to be the rebel, not
the goodie-goodie.

Food Not Bombs tonight. Super depressing. Old
lady on the bench, got kicked out of her house, hard
to tell if it happened two months ago or ten years
ago. Didn't know what to do. "I just got to find this
piece of paper. Then they'll give me my key." And
not sure if she's on the streets because she's crazy,
or crazy from being on the streets. Not sure what to
do either way. I was thinking about how there's
nothing short of bringing her back to the house that
I could do, facing the fact that I wasn't willing to do
that. I looked up at the White House, like a postcard
picture in the spotlights. I saw a huge rat in the
flowers, galloping away like a fucking dog.

Everyone is out tonight. Jordana and Christa
went to a women's coffeehouse meeting thing. Not
sure where Sean and Mike and Ed are. Read an old
issue of *Riot Grrrl* that had Christa and Jordana's
writing.

Things I need to do
1. Write more. (A zine?)
2. Go to shows alone. Or invite other
people to do shit, not wait to find out

what the house is doing.

3. Kiss someone. 87 and 1/2 days.

Can't even read *Riot Grrrl* without getting horny. Oy yoy yoy.

Michael's such a dick. Today he came in and was snacking on all the bulk foods. Susan was trying to look really happy and it was just really painful. "Smile and the world smiles back," he said to her. Sean made a puke face behind his back and Susan just kept smiling. Her face looked broken. I wasn't sure if she was going to cry or spit. When Susan got off, we were all hanging out by the register.

> Susan: "It should be illegal to schedule a place like this."

> Sean: "What, making people work here for more than 40 hours a lifetime?"

> Susan: "No, setting it up so that we all work seven and half hour shifts and can't get a lunch break or insurance or whatever cause we're not full time."

> Sean: "It's a health food store, just eat a lot of food, you won't get sick."

> Susan: "Michael's already on my ass enough, he'd probably fire me."

Sean was dropping a jar of garlic-stuffed olives into Susan's backpack while she was looking at me. Three seconds later, Michael came back in, "Come on guys, there's always something to do around here, no reason to be sitting around. I'll be in back getting ready to close."

Close call.

Feels shitty, making plans to become a lousy employee. At Wilson Video I wouldn't even take home the new releases because I wanted to keep the selection good for customers. But on the other hand, I could take home any other video for free with Mr. Roberts' blessing. Country mouse in the big city.

Long Distance, thank g-d.

Me: I'm going to shows, have a job, doing Food Not Bombs, cool friends, people are making their own magazines...

Them: Well, make sure to keep up with the writing and reading "so you won't be out of practice when you get to college."

Oy, yoy, yoy.

I thought statements from family therapists were supposed to be along the lines of "I hear what you are saying, and I support you in your efforts to become the person you want to become." At least Mom's capable of leaving her work at the office.

I thought your motto was "Tune in, turn on, drop out." Oh wait, maybe that policy has been revised to "Don't do what you want, go to college."

He looks to be about 18, wearing clothes that pretend to be picked without a thought as to fashion. Not quite tall, but posture that looks like he's used to ducking or accustomed to teachers and parents reminding him to sit and stand straight. He's got fast eyes, like he's new to this world, which he is. The kind of kid who finds a joke that pleases the crowd and keeps with it far beyond funny, as if to remind himself and the group that he has been capable of funny.

They're going bowling, and he seems confused, because bowling is old and familiar terrain, but these kids hate, loathe his old and familiar terrain.

So did Elliot, that's why he sought these new friends. But now they're going bowling, and it was the old Elliot that was the bowler. The new Elliot laughs out loud at the idea of bowling team. But these kids love to wear the shoes, and now they all have bowling names. Gilda and Bubba and Flamer are having a blast playing this goofy game, drinking soda, they even make a bet on the final score. Then the old Elliot comes to bowl, and the old Elliot wins the game by an easy 80 pins. And Christa ("Gilda" when she wears bowling shoes) is the big loser, so must karaoke at the Waffle House to the song of Elliot's choice (the old or the new, whichever shows up). And though he's realized that he's the dumb kid that's been invited to hang out only to be the butt of all the other's jokes, he doesn't see an even semi-graceful exit, and isn't hurt enough to look for revenge. So he acts as though he doesn't know, still hoping to win them over.

At the Waffle House he picks "Elvis Trilogy" and acts like Christa (Gilda) is really going to get up and sing along in the middle of the restaurant. He's trying to keep the lame trophy. And then seals his victory when the third part of "Elvis Trilogy" turns out to be "Dixie." "I wish I were in the land of cotton/ Old times there are not forgotten." He stops himself short of blushing, when he realizes that his eating partners haven't taken exception to the lyrics. During the rest of the meal, he's able to soothe his bruised ego by reminding himself that these kids don't even understand the racism of the song's words. It helps a little, but in the back of his mind he knows that they probably just weren't listening, probably just trying to pretend that the whole thing wasn't happening, that he wasn't there at all, ruining their night on the town.

And then, for a curtain call, he miscalculates his

part of the bill, so it looks like he is trying to leave an 18 cent tip.

The shittiest minutes of my DC.

Michael's latest cool move: keeping us late on Friday to clean store before remodeling, canceling work on Saturday so we don't even get O.T. Retaliation: free shitake mushroom and teriyaki sauce.

Me and Sean made dinner and everyone was psyched. At dinner, Sean said, "The sauce is compliments of Elliot's deep pockets, he's really coming along."

Everyone smiled and said thanks. Adda said, "Nice job, sauce liberator."

Nice to be patronized in your own home. At least there's one thing that my housemates don't think I'm a dork for doing.

Sean is working on a theft manifesto that he's going to make into a poster.

Ed's moving to Mt. Pleasant in October. I get his room. Housing dilemma solved.

More tired after my day off than before it. Drooling on the metro.

Hung out with Christa all day, chopped and cooked all evening, good rock show all night, up til dawn talking to Sandshark.

C asked me to a movie, maybe I'm not superdork after all. Pretty awkward, we'd been hanging out all day. I wanted to hold her hand, is she straight? single? into me? She's cool.

Tina came home. Mike in the living room in

underwear. Strange, everyone in the house being so nonsexual, and mostly shy. I was eating cornflakes, pretending to be reading. Tina has a road sign in her hands that says "Dingleberry Rd" and she's trying to tell him about how she stole it in Iowa.

Mike in his red briefs + Tina holding a sign that says "Dingleberry" = laughing, soy milk out my nose. It's a punk, it's a grocery store clerk, it's...SUPER NERD.

Haven't laughed like that since I moved to DC.

Then the big homecoming show. The same woman holding the dingleberry sign breathing fire. Tina rocks.

Christa has a Riot Grrrl stencil spray painted on the back pocket of her jeans. I stare at it a lot and then feel like a sleaze for staring at her butt. Then later I do it again.

Talking with her makes me think a lot. I can't tell if we're arguing or discussing. I guess we're both just really into what we're talking about. I always feel like our arguments are, on an unspoken level, about me being a sexist pig. I get defensive, but that could be because she's right. I don't know.

It's good to be challenged so that I think a lot about the words that I say and what they mean.

The bad part is: it's impossible to put the moves on someone when you are completely paranoid of them thinking you're a pig.

I can't believe how much bottled water we sell. People don't give a shit about what comes out of the faucets, as long as they can afford the clean stuff. Tough shit for the people who can't.

Eron invited me to work at Discontent stuffing copies of the new Colburn album, which is cool, meeting some new people, a little cash, and I'll get to see how it works. Amazing that he remembers me from TN. He and I both know that I remember him, cause I paid to watch and listen to him. But I'm amazed that he remembers me. Strange that across the world there are people that everyone will always remember and others that have to be psyched when those people remember them.

Came home, kids were all in the kitchen and living room Food Not Bombing. Talked to Colin on the phone. Hard to explain to someone at college what's going on here. Zines, music, politics, three local labels, everyone is up to something. Even the show tonight is raising money for a rape crisis center, not to mention it's all-ages. Feels like Haight-Ashbury in the 60's, except no one's doing drugs, or talking about sex (or doing it as far as I can tell). Plus, people don't have lice.

People who weren't the homecoming royalty and don't want to be.

Bored. But nothing seems like fun. Every record looks foreign and unpleasant to listen to, even my faves. Sick of reading, tv, music, walking and working. Feel like it's a Sunday and I'm dreading returning to school tomorrow. For no real reason, like it's just my time of month.

Haven't talked to Christa for a week. I can't tell if she's avoiding me. The last time I saw her we were at her place after the Three On The Tree show. Seemed obvious (to me) that I wanted to kiss her. She didn't say she was tired, I didn't offer to leave, she didn't invite me to stay, conversation wore thin. It was hard to tell what was up, or wasn't.

When I called tonight, Lisa said that she was out with Jonas. I wonder if they have something going. Jealous? Who me?

––––––––––

Maureen,

It's really good to get letters from you. I was laughin'. Are you sure that my parents don't pay you to write me about how great college is? You wouldn't believe the shit they've been giving me lately.

The other night I went to the Discontent House and helped package CDs and records for a big mailing. They do everything themselves, from promotion to tour, and they hire all these local punkers to work in the office and take care of various business things. It's pretty much the coolest business I've ever heard of. They're totally into documenting the DC punk scene, not putting out records just because they'll sell. The bands have total control over the music and covers, and the CDs never cost more than $8. I got paid $6 an hour to help, and got a free copy of the CD. It's awesome that there are people here who have gotten to the level of a nationally distributed record label, who keep going because they care about what they're doing, not because they're trying to make money. The idea of "rock stars" is pretty stupid, but I'm still in awe of the cool things they do.

A couple of nights ago I went to see a show at El Pollo Negro, the big club here, and in between the bands these women (part of the whole Riot Grrrl thing I told you about) were doing spoken word performance stuff. This woman who I think is super smart did a piece about beauty. I've been thinking about it a lot. I can't really summarize, but to summarize... It was about how men's perceptions of women's appearances, and women's awareness of the way that men look at them, are part of the violence that happens against women in our society. I feel like it was really good poetry no spare words and the words flipped around and felt different in each sentence.

The poem got me thinking about how annoyed you used to get when I told you that you were beautiful. Like on prom night. No matter how many times you told me, I never quite understood. I could try to remember, but then we'd end up in some situation where you looked great, and I'd be all giddy in love, and then I'd say it again.

The poem linked concepts of beauty and a culture of sexual abuse really well, and I finally understood a lot of things that you had been saying to me. I remembered the time that we were fooling around while the Springer's were on vacation, and I looked up after a while and you were crying. And feeling a wall that I hadn't known before between us. And I knew, somehow, that it was a wall that neither of us wanted, but one that we were going to spend a long time trying to get through or around, trying to feel close to each other again. And when you told me about that shit with your uncle, I knew that's what that day had been about, even though we've never talked about why you were crying. And now I understand a little more, maybe, about how you hated to hear about how pretty people think you are. It's pretty awkward to be writing this stuff, but seemed better than talking about it on the phone. I don't mean to just bring it up out of the blue, but it's stuff that I've been thinking about. Maybe you said some of the same things on prom night, in the midst of the Big Talk, and I just wasn't ready to understand. Feel like I'm starting to understand more of what went on between us. Which is cool.

I think a lot of crazy things about us. Sometimes I think that we'll never live in the same town again. Sometimes I'm scared that these letters are the epitaph. Sometimes I imagine our children, as they sort through our stuff, will find these letters, tied up with a dainty ribbon, and wonder if they should read them. It's all anchored securely in reality. (I especially like the idea of you wrapping the letters, reverently, with a yellow silk ribbon, the excess of the ribbon you used to make that darling Easter bonnet.) We're just simple country folk, doing the best we can, readin' the Bible, raisin' barns after they burn cause it was such a dry summer, and maybe a little dancin' after we harvest the crops. But not that kind of dancin'.

Take care, do your homework. Have fun with those kids at the grade school, Ms. Hall.

Your contact with what you Oberliners call "the real world," I am,

Elliot

Sorry if I went too far. I know we're supposed to be excited about these growing pains.

Got a raise at work. Think I'm supposed to be happy and go out to a big dinner with the wife. "That promotion finally came through, dear. We can afford our first child and the BMW."

"Oh love, I'm so proud of you. When you called and told me I went and put on your favorite lingerie." Woo hog.

Christa. I kissed Christa.

I kissed Christa and I really want to talk to someone about it. No one here who I can talk to about this kind of stuff. The person I really want to tell is still Maureen.

Tuesday night every one was over here and it was late. There was still stuff going on downstairs, so I offered my room. She was gonna sleep on the floor, but ended up in the bed, big enough for two. It was a long night of poor sleep and no action. A few days of total confusion, and now we've kissed.

In Wilson a kiss means this: we're going to date, be boyfriend and girlfriend. It means that we are going to walk around the mall with our hands in each others' back pockets. Cool that stuff here is more what we make it/ decide it to be. Not just plugging into premade roles that don't necessarily fit.

But being confused sucks. Maybe I'm just nervous.

Sean's manifesto is complete. A hard night of wheat-pasting pays off: *City Paper* ran a blurb about the poster. Pretty funny.

A suit came into the store today on lunchbreak, chatted it up with Sean. Made some joke about "those posters all over that say I should steal things." Sean said, "Go ahead." The guy looked kind of scared. As he left, Sean said loudly to me, "He certainly is a well-programmed one, isn't he?"

Ed says the phones were tapped when they organized protests last year and we should watch it, even with vandalism.

Official Notice by City Government of Washington, D.C.

STEAL EVERYTHING NOW

Top Ten Reasons Not To Pay

1. It's the American way. (You're standing on stolen land.)
2. Chain stores ruin small businesses. Big chains put more power in fewer people's hands. Theft makes these businesses less profitable and gives small business a chance.
3. Taking things without paying doesn't drive the cost up. Store owners already charge as much as the market will bear. That's how capitalism works.
4. It's like boycotting, except you don't have to do without.
5. Why should you do without just because you were born without?
6. If you don't pay, you won't need to work at jobs that suck, and you can do something meaningful with your time.
7. You could put that stuff to use. (Instead of letting it rot on the shelf.)
8. They charge too much.
9. Making capitalist ventures less profitable encourages people to do things more meaningful than selling junk to people who don't need it.
10. Sharing is good. Teach capitalists the value of sharing.

DON'T PAY.

All those found in violation will be ticketed

Haven't written in a while. Spending every other night with Christa, then too tired on nights alone. Not much to write. Go to work, eat food, make out, go to sleep. I like it fine. FNB on Saturdays, see some great bands, helping to set up a show. Every time that I see Christa around other people it's really weird, neither of us wanting to act couple-ish, or even treat each other different than our friends. So that sometimes, when we get into our bedrooms, it's hard to remember that we're supposed to be a couple. There are always a few minutes where I try to figure out if we are going to make out, or even hug. We never sneak into the bathroom to make out, and when we do make out it's not the hurry-up-and-touch-I-want-to-be-as-close-as-possible, it's more this-is-the-nice-thing-that-we-do-before-we-go-to-sleep. It's cool, because I feel like with her setting the pace, I never feel pushy or gross.

Going home tomorrow, and will see Maureen there. Christa asked "Is it going to be hard for her?" Guess that's her way of making it clear that we're not kissing other people. I guess it's unrealistic to expect to feel closer to Christa than to Maureen this early on.

Wonder what I'll tell Maureen about Christa.

Twelve hours driving with Jordana. We listened to a lot of seriously punk rock tapes.

As we got closer to home, Nauseous and I rode in the same seat, one low fare. When we rolled into town it was strange to be seeing all of this again, and stranger still knowing that another pair of eyes watched me and the town. Couldn't believe I was back; took less than two seconds to remember all the reasons that I left. Every building looked so po-dunk and stupid and third-rate, which was all right when we passed through the other small towns, but this one I knew. Knew just how rinky-dink and small the mentality is. I could already hear all of the questions (sincere) about what famous politicians and buildings I had seen. I could already hear Mrs.Bledsoe asking if I could get the president's autograph for her. And the stories about everyone's family trips to DC, and them acting like they know the town like the back of their hand. Not being able to explain that the only time I've been near the White House was to hand out food to homeless people.

With Jordana driving me it felt like I was in high school getting a ride home from some friend who I didn't want my parents to meet. Only I didn't want my friend to meet my hometown. And then I started to feel like Jordana represented everything that Mom and Dad are mad about in relation to me living in DC.

We pulled up in the driveway and walked through the door and I realized that it might be all in my head. M and D were happy to see me, I was happy to see them. Hannah and everyone was welcoming to Jordana and she smiled and didn't say much, but it didn't seem awkward. Little Sis was in rare form, a whole gaggle of things from school to show and various new talents to perform. When she saw Jordana's pink hair, she said, "Wow, what color is your parents' hair?" Everyone laughed and no one seemed to mind my new hairdo.

She's done this poem that goes:

> When you tell me to turn the page and
>   follow along with my finger,
> My stomach grumbles
> And I tell myself to eat a bigger breakfast
>   tomorrow.

I'm so happy about the poem that I want to hug her, but I've got my role. Plus she's thirteen and doesn't want to be hugged anyway, so we both stand there, awkward and happy.

Hannah assumes the role of interpreter and guide throughout the candle lighting. Gives play-by-play when the Guildensterns come over and all the people below the age of thirty five are required to play a game of dreidl so that Jordana can see How We Do It.

Jordana, the Pennsylvania anthropologist, scribbled page after page of notes, struggling mightily with the issue of how exposure was going to corrupt the authentic practices of our tribe. And a time was had by all.

Hard to go to sleep, knowing that I see Maureen tomorrow. Wish I could have seen her tonight. Strange that Jordana will be with us. Chaperone?

Seeing Maureen is insane. Wonderful. Horrible. Feel like I'm holding myself back from kissing her and holding her everytime no one is looking. Must be really obvious, too. I think she feels the same way. We watched *Over the Edge* at M's house. Jordana was asleep by the end (she's seen it about 100 times) and me and M were sort of cuddling.

When we left I felt like J thought I was a smutty boy who has different girls in each town and doesn't tell them about each other. Which isn't entirely true and isn't entirely a lie. I didn't do anything with Maureen that qualifies as Something I Have To Tell Christa About. And Maureen knows that I'm dating someone.

SO, <u>MINDCLEANER</u>. And a zine is born...

The other night my housemate Adda and I shaved our heads (1/4 inch) and then because we both looked so skinhead we made polka dots with bleach. And then I didn't look skinhead, but I did look ridiculous. Even though I'm all bad-ass and punk rock, I still felt embarrassed going to work in downtown DC with an uneven crewcut and sloppy bleach polka dots.

So now I'm writing this zine, and I have this big fear that it's going to turn out like my haircut. A lot of fun to make, but ridiculous and embarrassing. And oncethere's a hundred copies floating around the city, it will never grow out and turn back to its natural color.

It's much easier to talk- it's a huge luxury to have your words spoken, your ideas somewhat communicated and then gone. But writing things down is a good way to communicate ideas and information with people who you don't know. And it's important for us to document our ideas and lives, rather than let the mainstream media misrepresent us as "punks, lefties and freaks."

If you want more copies of thiszine, send some stamps. Otherwise, just pass it on, share it, send any letters/ articles/ care packages to:

PO Box 1666 Washington DC 20001
Your chance at literary fame awaits...

Thank you, thank you to everyone whose writing appears in this zine. I'm grateful that it's not all me.

Top of the Brain, errr, Somewhere in the non-hierarchical brain structure...

1. **Marchenko** live at United Presbyterian for $5 donation
1. **walkperson**- take the aural edge off many an unpleasantevent: Waiting for the metro while a mother slaps her kid around. Stocking yuppie natural foods. It's the ultimate technological antidote to depression. Especially with Blackmarket Clash playing.
1. **Food Not Bombs** lunches on Mondays, Wednesdays and Saturdays in Lafayette Square.
1. **Slacker**- the structure. The structure.
1. **BIKINI KILL** 12" and aldo live. + the name.
1. **Dreamy Tofu**-cheaper than ice cream and everyone in my house can eat it.
1. **Eros Auto Association** live at **DC Space**.
1. **House ofCurry's** all you can eat vegetarian lunch buffet- $2.99.
1. **Philadelphia Fire** by John Edgar Wideman. A novel about the bombing of the MOVE house in Philadelphia by the state police.The building caught on fire and the police snipers fired on anyone trying to leave the house. 11people died. 63 houses were destroyed. The story of a guy trying to figure out how and why it happened and how it relates to him.
1. **Krill,Amb.** Dont know how this 7 inch showed up in DC, but I'm glad.
1. **The Lazlo Letters**- Don Novello is a genius. He writes letters as though he's a big right wing kind of guyto all these right-wingers and corporationsand the he prints the letters along with the reply.
1. **Swimming to Cambodia**- Spalding Grey sits in a room and talks for an hour and a half and it's not boring. What college lectures are like in heaven.

Cash or Charge?

Cash or Charge? Pushing myself onward, past the abandoned old people on benches who await families to come claim them, wondering if they've been forgotten, their families already at home, trying to remember what they forgot to get at the mall. Past the kids being pushed and a slapped by their parents, kids who won't sit still long enough for parents to purchase the presents that prove their pride and love. Past the displays that whisper how lovely they would look smashed to pieces. Pushing through the crowd of sweatshirts with Christmas bows attached, ornaments that will be worn, then become the fur that insulates the interior of an ugly closet in an ugly house in an ugly suburb. Cash or Charge?

29.99

Would you like that wrapped? Past mothers and daughters who wait to get their claws manicured together. Makeovers so their warpaint will be properly festive for the occasion. Through a forest of poinsettias that will claim only slightly less landfill space next week. Close my nose to the airborn aroma of rain forest, fan blown into the mall, from the nature store, where I can buy some tiny momento of what used to live where we now splurge. Cash or Charge?

10.99

2.89

2/$5 1.99

1.79   99¢

79¢

Sale! 2/$1

Can I see your ID? Necklaces with your name engraved on a grain of rice. A bookstore where you can celebrate the birth of the messiah by purchasing books about nuclear subs chasing each other. Or perhaps you wanted a true-crime story?

One size fits all.

Cash or charge?
She looks at the diamond
ring that she so badly
needs and wonders how
she was saddled with the
kind of man who will
never be able to afford
to buy her one. And he
wonders what collection
of smaller, well-planned
purchases will distract
her from her lack of a
truly large diamond
ring? Cash or Charge?
Cash or charge?
Now, more than ever, I
want to charge, but I
know that the invitation
to charge holds a
painful, deadly sword
hidden, waiting for me.
I must pace myself, to
get at least one of my
horns into the flesh of
the tormentor before I
go.

Make It Home For The Holidays— Just Video Conference!

Sale!

Would you like $love?

XX A CASE STUDY OF THE "PUNK" REACTION by Tomothy

"charlie "comes from a middle class family. He was refer
redto me through family members who were concerned about
his obsessive cleanliness, bordering on obsessivene
ss. as he spoke he gesticualted wildly. Each visi
t was the same, as though he had been programmed to
give no more than an offer of initiation to the
enemy, and to deviate from the script would be trea
son. XX He was onlyunder my care xxfor one month
(four) visitsbefore he was killed beneath the wheel
s of a passing truck. What follows is a transcripti
ion of his second session (thoughagain all session
were identical) .

"How are you today, Charlie. Please have a seat,
or lay on the couch as you prefer."

"How am I? Let me tell you , how Ia m you fuck. Li
sten, some cats might be willing to sit around lick
ing themselves, acting like the world doesn't suck,
butI'm not. Fuck this. How am I?. Fed up, pissed
off. TIred ofg all the bullshit and tired of watchi
ng us sell out and become part of this shit. Look,
ixxm it's not rocket science. They're not smart.
We just have to know the score, then swipe with an
paw that hasn't been declawed.

POINT ONE. CORPORATE ROCK EQUALS DEATH. Not just
of the soul, but also of the living beings. When
Sonic Youthhas a hit record, each copy xxx sold
makes more money for a company that invests in
projects like computer systems that will launch the
remaining nuclear weapons in the arsenal after the
war (world) ixxixxk has been lost.

The way it used to be, we lived in small communitie
s and made art for each other as a natural expressi
on of our environment and culture. But now it's al
l about the dollakr, and you know that some exec
utive in a suit isn't gonna let some thing slide by
on artisitc maxmerrit, if he could even grasp that.

Like anything else, records hav eto make money.
It's not about passion for the music , it's a busin
esswith all the cold, heartless trappings of the
business world layering themselves on top of kernel
of real emotion and meaning that the artists in
tended to communicate. even people who continue to
try to say things axxwith meaning are packaged, on
Letterman to promotienal posters. What can be sadd
erthan watching Nirvana on the tonight Show sandwic
hedbetween commercials for Miller Genuine Draft

(yep the one with all the girls you'll get to sleep with ₫ if only you buy MGD) and Jeep CHerokee (yep the one with all the girls you'll get to sleep with if only you buy Jeₚₚ) When you sell your music you have to sell yourselfₓₙ, condense your thoughts and ideas for easy consumption. If you package yoursel f in to spin-magazine-interview sizeḏ responses to difficult, existential questons- eventually you bec ome that two dimmensional, black words onwhite page soulless person. which leads to...
AND POINT TWO- I;m sick of people who think they're hot shit because they can play music that could jus tas easily be an ad for fodder for the machine. Pe ople who ₚₖₐₓ play music are no better than anₜₒₙe else. This seems obvious, but it seems like a lot of people have forgotten. We should all be able to treat each other nicely, and it doesn't matter what wewear, who we know or what band we're in. Because , really, anyone can be in a bandn and should be if they want to .
 "And POINT /THREE, not only can we all be in bands , we can all set upₚ shows, write our own magazines and books, make our own art, and have ₒₕₖ o it benefit things that mean somehting real. Even if we jsut end up becoming closer to one another and making new friends, at leastwe're not g giving money to THorn EMI's production of MX missile componeḫts.
"We don't need the glitz and glamouṯ of some shitty magazinesand clubs who just want to increase alcohol sales. We can we can keep our art meaningf ul within our own communities, ₓ even if we have to recreate our ownculture. and instead of making more money to buy more ₓ useless crap, we go to good causes and things the we believe in like Food Not Bombs, the Rape Crisis Center or the SPCA."
     "Listen some cats might be too stupid to sprea d a little sand around in the litter box after they take a shit, but I'm fed upwith it. "
Four paws on the ground no goodbyes and out the door.

RIOT HERE RIOT NOW

Listen up girls! There's a new gang in town,
and it's all about love, girl-love, self love,
love grrrrl style.. Cuz we're sick of looking
at the back of boys' heads at punk rock shows to
see some sweaty boys on stage. Are you sick of it
too? Are you sick of being interrupted in conversati
ons by boys who are supposedly your friends?
(You don't interrupt them that much, do you?)
Sick of being asked by those boys to hold there jack
ets while they slamdance at shows? As if you aren't
there cuz you want to see the band too, as if you
could stand up front and see the band without getting
knocked over by sweaty, slamdancing boys. (Just
because we have the courtesy not to kick those
'boys' asses, not cuz we can't do it.)

Special Listen Up Section for Boys:

DOMINANT CULTURE EXISTS IN THE PUNK SCENE. If you
don't think so it's because you aren't constantly
made aware of it. Figure out why that is.
Punk rock is supposed to be about doing it
yourself, and creating a better society, not
conforming to existing, crappy patterns.
So what is this sexism crap in punk?!?! There's
no place for that, but how can we stand up and
fight it if we don't support each other with girl
love?

How many times have you been told that you're not
so great, and in how many ways in the "punk"
scene? Like those boys are so great because they
play in their mediocre bands or they do their zines,
so that the punk scene, like the rest of the world,
will be saturated with the narrow opinions of men
on issues of interest to men, or shall we say BOYS
Punk started as a reaction against our culture being
controlled by someone else. When is punk culture

going to be controlled by all who are actually in it?
It's time for GRRRL culture!

But Riot Grrrrl isn't just about punk, it's about
taking control of all parts of ████ our lives..
It's about making every one that you encounter
understand that you, and all women, deserve
respect and that you're not g ing to do what
someone else wants, just because it's ex█xxxx
expected of you. FUCK EXPECTATIONS... Fuck being
told that we have to like boys, that we have to be
nice (even though others █x don't have t be nice
to us) fuck being told that we have to get
married or go to school, or anything!! Riot Grrrl
is about us taking control of ███ our own lives
and telling other people what we will do. And
that means that we ███ e ach get to decide what's
right for us, not having the patriarchy or the
 punktriarchy dictate how we spend our time, or who
we spend it with. You can come to Riot Grrl
meetings in the DC area. We talk about all of
this tuff and so much more. You can meet other
people who want to be in bands with you, to
make movies with you, to make zines with you; to
meet ██ people who want to support you in whatever
you are doing, because women don't get █x e█x enough
support and it's time we start supporting each
other. You can call 703 564 GRRL to find out about
the next meeting. (every other week, usually. the l
location changes. GRRRLS ONLY! safe space)

You can send $1 to Riot Grrrl Publications,
PO Box 453, WDC, ██ 20030 for a grab abg of grrrl
zines, including the █x "riot grrrl" zine.

Send us your zine, and we can make copies and
distribute them to other grrrls all over the world.
If you don't live near DC, you can start your own
Riot Grrrl group. Don't worry about doing it right
or wrong, just get together and talk about █what
 YOU need to talk about!!!

                          -Christa

Eros Auto Association

interview by Sagit

Washington DC's Eros Auto Association have just released an LP on Discontent records, entitled 10 Easy Steps to Revolution. The record is a crazy mixture of energy, music, political rhetoric and what they call "the jazz of rebellion, the rebellion of jazz." In their liner notes, they claim to "speak for those who the man tries to saddle with age." I spoke to Tina Chromwell(bass, vocals) and Aaron Pavapolous (vocals, blueprints) at their first show back in D.C. after a two month tour.

Lincoln
196x

M(e): How was tour?
T(ina): Well Canada was pretty lame. The shows in America went well.
A(aron): (while writing "fight back" on his fist) American Youth feel the need for liberation. They've saved room in their lives.

M: How did you guys form?
T: Well I've been friends with Aaron for...
A: We formed out of necessity. We were transformed from friends to political party to separatist movement. We are youth, and have proclaimed all of our ages to be 18, eternally.

Fiat
1957

T: I'm 18, long live youth.
M: In the liner notes of your new album, you refer to a lot of bands and people as "republics" including Marchenko and Riot Grrrl. How does that tie in to what you're trying to do as a band?
A: We're using music as our medium because we know it's the only thing kids give a shit about. We're a terrorist group, like the Black Panthers or the IRA.

T: We're trying to do something different than just put out records and make music.

M: What is that?

A: We're trying to strike the man dead.

T: Each song is strategically designed for maximum killing potential...

Plymouth
1957

A: We test it, then unleash it on the public, they're all smart bombs, they strike only those who need to be hurt. Each one has castrating potential, but youth can receive the shocks again and again, we'll twist and undulate, but emerge triumphant and unscathed. Each song attacks a different problem, right now we operate in an aural field, each member of the association wields their weapon with care.

T: I play bass.

A: We attack now, aurally. In the future the arrows of Eros may be more literal than figurative. Force. For now we've allied ourselves with the forces of chaos, because chaos is far superior to the structure of mediocrity, which is the man.

M: Does the plan call for more records?

T: This spring, ten inches of micro-grooved revolution.

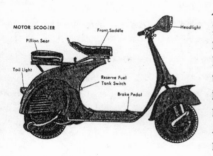

MOTOR SCOOTER

Pillion Seat

Front Saddle

Headlight

Tail Light

Reserve Fuel
Tank Switch

Brake Pedal

A: A front, camouflage for the guerrilla war on the power structure. Play the record, and the weapons of the man can harm us not.

M: Like the ghost shirt?

A: On Discontent, with all the articles we've assembled since the last communiqué.

Ford
1957

SMASH THE STATE
SABOTAGE THE PHONE CO.

EVERYBODY KNOWS THAT PHONE COMPANIES HAVE THEIR FINGERS IN JUST ABOUT EVERY EVIL PIE, FROM NUCLEAR WEAPONS TO PRICE FIXING TO DEFORESTATION. PLUS IT ONLY COSTS THEM MONEY TO LAY THE PHONE CABLES ONCE, SO WHY DO WE HAVE TO PAY AND PAY? DO YOURSELF AND EVERYONE ELSE A FAVOR, MAKE YOUR CALLS FOR FREE. HERE'S HOW:

STEP #1 BUILD A DIALER.

BUY A "33 MEMORY TONE DIALER" FROM RADIO SHACK. USING A SCREW DRIVER, CAREFULLY REMOVE THE BACK OF THE DIALER. SAVE THE SCREWS. FIND THE SILVER CYLINDER ON THE LEFT THAT READS "3.55." DESOLDER THIS CYLINDER, AND REPLACE IT WITH ONE THAT READS "6.5536." WRAP NEW CYLINDER IN TAPE, REPLACE BACK COVER OF DIALER AND PUT THE SCREWS BACK. CHIPS CAN BE BOUGHT BY CALLING 1-800-DIGIKEY. ASK FOR A 6.5536 MHz TIMING. TRY TO BUY CHIPS ENOUGH FOR YOU AND ALL YOUR FRIENDS AT ONCE.

STEP #2 PROGRAM THE DIALER

SWITCH THE "DIAL/STORE" BUTTON TO "STORE" THEN PRESS THE "MEMORY" BUTTON, THEN PRESS "*" FIVE TIMES, THEN PRESS "P1." SWITCH THE "DIAL/STORE" BUTTON BACK TO "DIAL" AND YOU ARE ALL SET.

STEP #3 MAKE FREE PHONE CALLS

Ⓐ FIND A PUBLIC PAYPHONE Ⓑ DIAL THE LONG DISTANCE # THAT YOU WISH TO CALL, AS IF YOU WERE GOING TO USE COINS TO PAY THE CHARGES Ⓒ HOLD THE SPEAKER ON THE DIALER DIRECTLY AGAINST THE MOUTHPIECE OF THE RECEIVER, PRESS "P1" FOR EACH QUARTER REQUIRED Ⓓ REPEAT STEP C WHEN THEY ASK AGAIN FOR MONEY.

THINGS TO REMEMBER

THE SOUND THAT YOUR DIALER (WITH A NEW CHIP) MAKES WHEN YOU PRESS THE "*" BUTTON IS THE SAME SOUND THE PHONE MAKES WHEN IT CREDITS THE USER FOR A NICKEL. YOU HAVE PROGRAMMED "P1" TO BE THE SOUND OF FIVE NICKELS, (ONE QUARTER). THE PHONE CO. CANNOT TELL YOU ARE USING A DIALER, AND IF THEY SOMEHOW FIGURE IT OUT, THE CALL CAN ONLY BE TRACED TO A PAYPHONE. DON'T USE THE SAME PHONE ALL THE TIME. IF A LIVE OPERATOR COMES ON LINE, ASKING FOR MONEY, USE REAL CHANGE. OR HANG UP.

Wilson, Tenessee, Bithplace of
Elliot the Bar-Mitzvahed and a heck of a
place to play football and get in fights:
   Pilgrimage is more than the name of an
   REM song

     I waited for darkness, to hide my shame
and sin. Even the setting of the sun hid
me not, for the sky in the South was aglow.
I knew that I could stay away no longer. It
was time for the first return of the prod-
igal son.
     Across the desert of Virginia, to that
golden city lit by the glow of a million
Chanukah lights sped Jordana and I. Each
December, like Harley riders to Sturgis,
like mosquitos to the zapper, the Jews of
the world pilgrimage to Wilson, Tennessee.
And thus, December 16th found me riding shot
gun, as Jordana the Christian and I brought
the sacred olive oil to the expectant throng
assembled in Wilson's town square.
     At the gates of the city we paid our
respects to the village elders, making sure
our camels decelerated through the radar-
enforced speed trap. At the den of the
elder Rosenbergs we were greeted with hugs
and that kosher vegan treat- potato latkes
with applesauce.
     The fires were lit, the prayers
chanted, the food prayed over and eaten.
We sat with the elders, recounted the journey
from the big city and it was good. Dreidl
was the next order of business, and there is
only one place in Wilson with a standing
dreidl game.
     To Smiley's Pool Hall, the den of ini-
quity, where to our enormous surprise we
found Jay, Colin and all begatten in 1970-
74. Colin and Jay were involved in the

World Series of Billiards (Jay wins =
anarchist society, governed by individual
good will and love, is possible. Colin wins
= humanity is inherently flawed and needs
leadership.) We arrived in game seven,
in which Colin took it all when Jay sunk the
eight and then the cue ball. Jay, upon
losing began to sulk and converse with Emma
Goldman and Hakim Bey, eventually working up
such fervor that he bumped into Lionel at
the next table. The whole affair was settled amicably with a few dozen punches and
a gross of "fuck you"s.

On the ride home I had to explain some
of the ancient rituals still performed in
Wilson, such as the sacred "cleansing of the
body after two males make contact" dance that
had been performed at Smiley's. Jordana,
although well traveled, seemed surprised that
life in Wilson still revolved around such
primitive activities.

And weighty upon my mind was an image of
the tapestry of all the tiny lives and inter-
actionsthat is WIlson TN. It grieved me
greatly to see my companions laid low, indeed, by the daily occurrences of the town.
BUt most seem fairly content. I asked the
powers, with my mind's mouth, what was to be
done for those who chose to dwell in darkness.

On the way home, we stopped to refuel
the camels at the Exit 181 oasis. While
Jordana took care of the gas pump, I found
the restroom. Upon my return to the camel,
I noticed a bush afire, burning brightly
without being consumed. Closer inspection
revealed it to be a shrubbery cloaked in
Christmas lights in the gas station median.
Nevertheless, the electric bush did speak,

and this is the question it asked:
    "Hast thou moved to DC to be around
deviants in the hopes that you can learn to
'deviate from the norm' correctly? Willst
thou purport that thou livest the revolution
when it isn't all around you? If thou cannot
be punk rock in Wilson, thne is it truly
radical to be radical in DC? Willst thou
keep the revolution quiet?"

    When I'm not in Wilson, I feel like I
need to go back and tell everyone that when
they're sitting in their easy chairs,
watching TV and going about their lives,
they're still actively supporting a government
that terrorizes and murders. They're paying
taxes that fund programs that kill people
and imprison them and make people sick and
destroy people's homes and lives. And these
programs are given the okay, the go-ahead by
people who are suppopsedly responsible to us.
    But then when I get to Wilson, I feel
like a fanatic with a bible in my hand,
knocking on the door, saying get out of
your easy chairs, get away from your television, come to the church of the radical and
be saved.
    I guess most don't see it. When things
are o.k. for you, you want to think that you
earned it. When the government creates problems for you, it's often more than you can
do just to deal. Sometimes I wonder why I
see it, why bushes talk to me in parking lots.

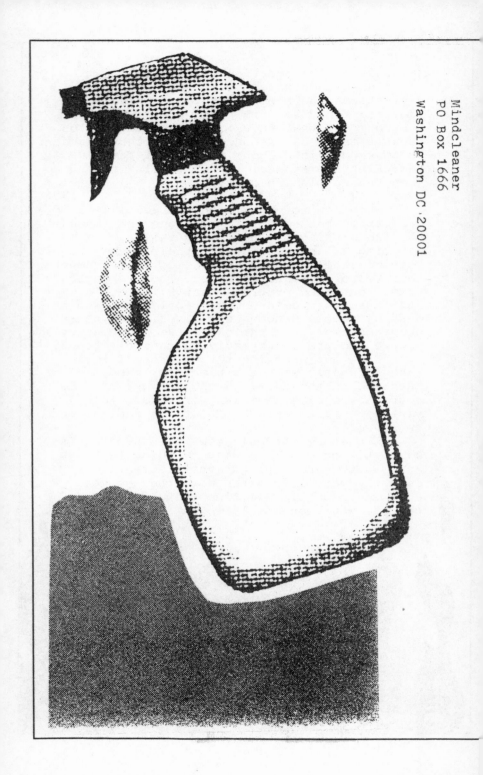

Mindcleaner
PO Box 1666
Washington DC 20001

Looks like the house that Tomothy and I have been scheming about really might happen. There's a meeting here tomorrow. The idea was a house that also was a community space, and when we first started talking about it, it seemed good but far-fetched, but now that we've been talking about it for a while.

Inga, T.K. and this guy Matt who Tomothy knows all said they might live in a place with us. I guess T.K. and Matt helped start FNB here, now they do Anarchist Black Cross stuff.

———

Not really in the mood to write. Still sort of worried about last night.

Last night in bed I asked if we should get some condoms and she seemed really flustered. Cool with me if it didn't happen, but then I felt like a jerk for bringing it up. "What's wrong?" "Nothing." Nothing-nothing, or don't-want-to-talk-nothing? Just a single word, a back turned.

Awake most of the night wondering what was going on. Did I fuck up by asking about sex so soon (two months)? Did she think I was trying to pressure her? Is she afraid of diseases/pregnancy? Is she having sex with other people?

When she woke up in the morning she acted like nothing had happened. I already felt gross about last night, didn't want to make her more uncomfortable. Wish I could read her mind.

———

Still don't know what was going on the other night. She seemed happy tonight. We had fun. Guess she doesn't hate me. It seems like no talk is good talk with Christa when it comes to sex.

I'm pretty sure her Mom and Dad are pissed

about her dating me. Maybe it's the Jewish thing. Says her family has "great respect for the Jewish faith" but if you have to say something about it... Maybe they think we're having sex, which they're probably upset about, and it looks like I'm treating their daughter like a tramp by doing it with her and then not spending the holidays with her. Like they'd be psyched if she had gone to TN with me... Not much fun dating a whole family. Wish Christa stood up to her folks as much as she stands up to me.

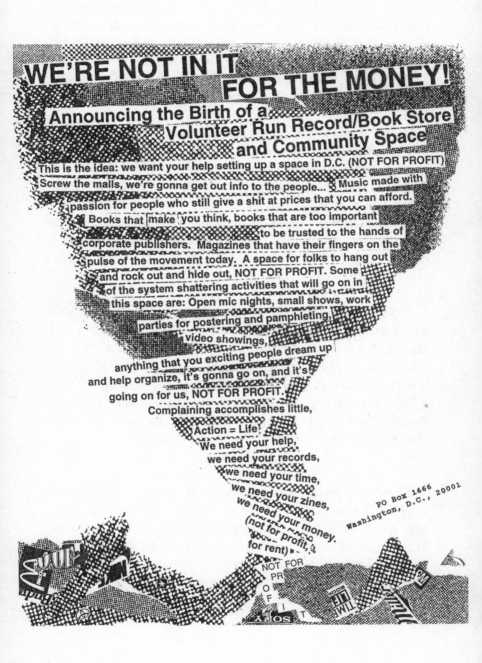

WE'RE NOT IN IT FOR THE MONEY!

Announcing the Birth of a Volunteer Run Record/Book Store and Community Space

This is the idea: we want your help setting up a space in D.C. (NOT FOR PROFIT) Screw the malls, we're gonna get out info to the people... Music made with passion for people who still give a shit at prices that you can afford. Books that make you think, books that are too important to be trusted to the hands of corporate publishers. Magazines that have their fingers on the pulse of the movement today. A space for folks to hang out and rock out and hide out, NOT FOR PROFIT. Some of the system shattering activities that will go on in this space are: Open mic nights, small shows, work parties for postering and pamphleting, video showings, anything that you exciting people dream up and help organize, it's gonna go on, and it's going on for us, NOT FOR PROFIT. Complaining accomplishes little, Action = Life! We need your help, we need your records, we need your time, we need your zines, we need your money. (not for profit, for rent)

PO Box 1666
Washington, D.C., 20001

NOT FOR PROFIT

Last night Christa and I were fooling around in my bedroom. It was getting intense. She asked where the condoms were. It caught me a little off guard, but I got them out, and asked if she was sure. "Yeah," she said. "I mean it makes sense at this point." (Riot Grrrl speak for "Take Me, I'm Yours!")

I was pretty psyched, but then had trouble with the condom and had to get out another. Then we did it and it kept stopping and starting and falling out. Seemed like a struggle. It was awkward, not in a cute, tee-hee way, but grim, let's-take-care-of-this-business. It was like she didn't want to be in charge and get on top, but didn't like me being on top of her.

Psyched. Looks like Hornets Nest will happen. Matt and T. K. and I signed the lease. On the bus I felt like we were a couple who just got married and got a real "fixer upper." Couldn't wait til T and I got home, to tell them. So much stuff to do.

Need to talk with Jordana, to make sure that she doesn't want one of the rooms. To make sure that she knows that I'm sad to be leaving her.

The tension makes you sick to your stomach, or maybe it's not the tension, maybe it's the disgusting grocery store cake you convinced me to buy. Whatever the reason, you don't want to eat anymore. Now that I'm hungry, I can't even enjoy it. Your housemates will eat the cake now, they won't thank me, they don't like me because I always make you cry.

Psyched. Jordana asked me to be in a band. Can't think of anyone else I'd want to be in a band with, and I'll be less lonely cause I'll get to talk to her a lot.

We need a drummer and maybe a bassist, although Jordana plays bass and guitar, and when she plays her guitar through the bass amp, it sounds pretty heavy, and good. So maybe just a drummer.

Super Vixen's visit to the house was overload for everyone. These guys show up, find out they can't drink in the house, so they get wasted and sleep in the front lawn. Super punk rock. Fun and breaking rules. And they weren't assholes. They played an all ages show and respected the rules of our house, but still had fun. Now everyone hates them, but can't even really talk about the incident because it didn't involve someone being "insensitive to issues." Just a lot of snide comments about "cool punk rockers." "Oh, you guys are so '77." etc. They just wish they could have fun too, but they can't remember how.

I hope I can.

It seems like all anyone does in this house is talk about "problems." And then more problems arise because of what people say when they're talking about problems. There's always some kind of mis-understanding or someone misrepresenting what someone else said. Analysis paralysis. But if I don't want to talk then I'm being insensitive.

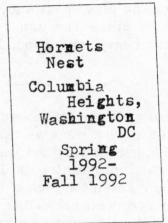

Hornets
Nest

Columbia
     Heights,
Washington
          DC
Spring
1992-
Fall 1992

Moved out of P.C. house today. Had the urge to smoke a cig, eat a burger, shoot some smack, read some porn. But the fact that I could do any of this stuff and not get yelled at by my housemates suddenly made it seem unappealing again. Ahhh, freedom.

Hornets Nest. More like Dirt Dobber Central. All dirt all the time. Everything I own is going to be coated in grime soon.

---

3 a.m. - Spray cans, backpacks, stencils. Out to eliminate nazi graffiti. Painting over "SS" and swastikas, not talking about it, making months of plans. One person decides, invites others to help, then we're doing it. No meetings.

Great to have housemates who will drop everything to make stencils that have pictures of the members of Kiss to cover up the "SS" shit with "KISS." Nice to have fun doing something important and also break the law and also paint pictures of Gene Simmons all over town. Just realized how awesome it is, considering that Gene and Paul are Jews. Fucked up that nothing happened to the person who wrote "SS" all over town, but we'd go to jail if we get caught painting over it.

First practice. Noodled around on our guitars and talked about possible drummers. Annoying that I don't know the words or the names of all the chords. Which was no big deal when we were just playing around and not trying to remember any of it. But now we're trying to repeat the cool things that happen.

"That was cool, when you were playing that A, C, A and I was doing the opposite."

"Huh?"

"You know, when I was doing this."

And when she does it again, I know what she's talking about and I can replay my part. Then we give it names. Our first song goes, "Sonic Youth Part, Jewish Summer Camp Part, Sonic Youth Part, Marchenko Plays the Sonic Youth Part Part, Jewish Summer Camp Part." And we can play it. Now for drums, someone who knows what we mean when we say, "Marchenko Plays Sonic Youth Part Part."

I want to be close to people who call me on the stupid things that I say or do, I want them to have high standards for me, but sometimes it seems like things with Christa are about me being constantly corrected. She does bring up things that I wouldn't necessarily think about. She brought up heterosexual privilege, I think mostly because I touched her waist when she came into the store yesterday. She talked about how other people have to constantly worry about the consequences of their touches. And we're lucky that we don't.

But a lot of times I don't think that we're arguing about language or power dynamics as much as she doesn't trust me at all and is just waiting for me to show my true, evil self. When do we get to stop trying to prove ourselves and just enjoy each other's company? Of course Christa would say that it's in my interest and not hers to let our guards down. Why does she want to hang out with me if she's really worried that I'm so conniving? Maybe this is how relationships really work (and often don't)Oy yoy yoy.

April 22, 1992

Hannah,

Happy Birthday. What's one to say? 729 days of Hannah-free driving left in Tennessee.

I just moved into a new place- in the city, as I'm sure that M and D have told you. It's crazy, me and five other people are all crammed into this building that's designed to be retail space. We're going to make the downstairs into a record store/ book store/ place for meetings, and we'll live upstairs. I've got a nice "office," formerly the Omega Tax Preparation headquarters.

Even though the house is super dirty, I'm excited about it. Everyone that lives here is really cool, and they're all into political action. Two guys started the DC chapter of Food Not Bombs, a group that gives out healthy food for free three times a week and at political rallies. And there's Inga, from Belgium, who helped turn this abandoned house into a bookstore and place for kids to live. I'm finally around the people that I hoped to be around when I left Wilson.

The neighborhood is called Columbia Heights. It's mostly a Black and Latino area. Right now, most of the stores around us are liquor stores and check-cashing places that sell Lotto tickets and stuff like that, but we're right by a new Metro stop, and a bunch of more "upscale" cafes and stores are starting to open up down the street.

We're going to try not to be "upscale" like that, because when the neighborhood starts becoming more of a shopping area for people with more money, the rent will go up and a lot of people who live here might not be able to stay. Even us punks being around could be part of the problem. White people (even smelly punkers) added to the landscape makes yuppies from the suburbs feel safer and increases property value. It sucks, and it happens a lot in big cities. We're hoping that we can use some of the energy and money of the punk kids to do something cool here. So far it's mostly meetings and painting and cleaning, but fun. I'm in charge of the book store end of things. It's a lot of work, but I get to scour thrift stores for good books.

I'm in a band. It's me on guitar and Jordana on bass and guitar and this guy Sagit on drums. Sagit is still in high school and we practice at his folks' house. I like finally playing music with other people. I'm used to playing silly songs for you and Maureen. Oh and Jordana says hi and happy birthday.

M and D seem pretty unpleased about the move, especially since I'm committed to being here for a while, which means more Not Attending College in my near future. It's sucky to be turning out so foreign to them, especially since I feel like I'm who I am (whatever that is) because of what they taught me to be. I feel lucky to have had them for parents, and I wonder and hope they feel the same about how I'm "turning out." Urrgh. What I mean is that I love them and I hope that they're ok with all of this. Maybe they're totally fine about all of this, and the only strain is when the Joneses come over for bridge and high tea and inquire how I'm doing at college and they have to explain what I'm doing...

They've been cool about everything. I just wish that they had dreamed for me to start a really cool collective in DC. Which is more than any kid can rightly expect. Listen to me lament, while so many of the kids I hang out with have parents who beat them up and worse.

We're really lucky. Which ain't to say that everything's perfect, but we're definitely lucky.

I hope things are still going okay in Wilson. Write

me another letter soon, please. Your stories about school are funny. Give my love to mom and dad, but you don't need to tell them about the rats in my basement.

Love,
Elliot

Adrenaline.

You fly by the cameras, disguised as white rich kids, no one suspects you and you strike. Not a real blow, nothing that will tear down any walls, but you will create a diversion. The heart you feel beating in your throat and the sweat on your palms, you know how a risk feels, and you know that you have to trust yourself and this is good training. You walk through a wall and all the while a million excuses and lies go through your head, and then you come out on the other side. Now you're ready to think up bigger excuses, bolder moves, thicker walls.

There's absolutely no one watching. So why not? A pocket full of candy, a shirt full of books, an armload of t-shirts. And while they scramble to set up a new camera, to keep an eye on someone else, you hit behind their back. When everyone is suspect, the searches and evil eyes will be on us all, more freedom for some, a taste of being watched for those who think that they are free in the marketplace.

What we really need is a bunch of people dressed as church ladies to pull the biggest heist Kmart has ever seen. A bunch of guys in three piece suits to get caught with crap in their pockets. But they won't get caught, they'll get praised, they'll get a history textbook written about them, their conquest, just lift that land right from under someone's feet. Someday we'll build a Kmart there and charge them for all the stuff that we say they need. Plastic shoes, popcorn poppers, and, of course, TVs (how else can you find out about all the stuff that you need?).

The people with the longest histories of stealing still have the most freedom to roam through the store, unwatched. My founding fathers stole the land that this place sits on, so I can pay for this shit if you want. Here, have a few green tickets.

———————

During graffiti correction strike #2, bumper sticker: "Visualize World Peace."

Visualize world peace? Maybe we can visualize paying our rent this month and see if the landlord can tell the difference. Maybe I'll just visualize going to work from now on instead of actually going and see if I still get paid.

Visualize world peace? Get off your ass and DO something for world peace you hippie fuck.

The car looks much nicer now.

———————

Fuck. Here I sit, writing my zine. Letters from prisoners come in. How did they get copies? Wish I'd thought to send copies. Thinking of all the shit we do that's not legal.

"Make sure to take the staples out, and take out pages that have directions of how to do anything illegal. Make sure to address the envelope to my prisoner number, as packages with names instead of numbers get thrown out. Send stamps if you can, please. I can't always afford to write back otherwise."

Article in the paper today: 18 year old girl sentenced to life for selling LSD. Article on page two: Maryland man gets 2 years for killing his wife. Meanwhile I'm thinking about the logistics of getting a P. A. for a punk rock show and renting a church basement. Marchenko say they'll play a Food Not Bombs benefit if I set it up. Some days it feels like giving away free food is just fattening up the turkeys for the slaughter. Just keeping everyone healthy enough to eventually be useful in the work camps. But what can you do?

I'm sure it's illegal to have shows in a basement and charge money. Tax evasion. It's illegal to give away food that's about to be thrown away. To call it a conspiracy might be giving too much credit, but the actuality looks evil enough.

Mechanically making out. Knowing that it's not going to be too pleasing to me, thinking she just does it to please me. Feeling like it's never that pleasing to her. Maybe we'll get through this and passion will return. If we stop and talk about it, things will be broken beyond repair.

She starts getting really aggressive. Hmmm.

She says, "Let's get out a condom."

While I fumble around under the mattress, the phone rings. Mariana yells, "It's for you, Christa." She grabs pants and shirt off the floor. Through the door I hear her talking about zine things- columns, letters, distro- it goes on for 24 and 1/2 minutes.

She comes back in the room, looks at me lying naked on the bed, seems puzzled, as if she can't remember who I am. I look at her for a minute, stand up. Left leg, then right leg, zipper. Socks, shoes, laces, shirt in hand, gone. No words.

Now I understand. You "can't be in a heterosexual relationship in a patriarchal society." And that's why you wanted to make sure that I had severed all ties to Maureen. That's why you didn't want Maureen and I to hang out for a night when I was in Wilson, because you didn't want to be in a heterosexual relationship with me. Makes perfect sense. What? Fuck you. Leave me alone. Fuck you.

You're crying and you could walk and cry but you just want to cry on the stoop where all my friends are inside working on planning a neighborhood financial counseling workshop. And then you say "You just wanted to use me to do dirty things, you didn't even like me."

And temper I didn't know I had.

And then I'm yelling, because it's so ridiculous, because I'm dealing with someone who thinks that kissing and sex is dirty which is...

And also that I was only in it for the sex when all I fucking wanted was things to be happy or something.

And then I'm on the stoop, mid-yell, and I know that I'm one of those lousy parents that you see dragging their kid behind them on the subway, or that parent who wears a walkman while their kid screams on the bus, and you wonder who let them have kids, or aren't they even embarrassed by what shitty parents they are.

And T.K. and Inga and Tomothy inside, wondering if they should call child protective services, but there's really no easy answers.

"Some people should never be allowed to have children."

"Dirty things."

I wonder if you're only allowed to become famous if you have nothing to say, or if fame becomes the point, and what else is there to say, except, "I'm famous." Perhaps a little charity work, but not for anything too far beyond the Red-Cross.

Or if we tune you out if you spend too much time talking about "issues."

> After you make the winning touchdown
> Imagine all eyes on you
> You just won it all
> You can say whatever you want
> Reporters arrive
> And you don't say, "All Glory to God"
> You don't say, "Viva La Raza"
> You don't say, "I love you mom and Dad"
> You don't say, "Thank you"
> You do say, "I'm going to Disneyland,"
>   and you make some cash
> And little kids, as they make their half
>   court shots, say "3, 2, 1... bzzzz"
> And begin mouthing your important
>   words

Wonder what Aaron P. or Tina will do when they get famous. What they'll say. Wonder if they'll still be babbling about how they're terrorists and their songs are bombs. When are you really famous? How many kids have to buy your records before you're a rock star? At what point does it matter if you're saying anything or not? At El Pollo Negro? On MTV?

———————

May 29, 1992

Maureen,

Your letter made my week. Research for $14 an hour? Beats the shit out of Wilson in June, July and August. Hope you don't get bit by any radioactive spiders. Also, check for insects before teleporting. Seriously, though, congrats. It sounds rad.

Can't believe that shit you wrote about the bike derby. It takes an average SAT score of 1300 to come up with that kind of shit. I especially like the part where everyone left the bicycles and compost piles for the groundskeepers to clean up. Must be hard to discuss Melville with someone who you've seen covered in beer, flinging compost at groundskeepers. Lifestyles of the rich and intellectual, so charming.

So here's issue number two. Let me know what you think.

By the way, I'm in a band, got tired of seeing people on stage, so I decided I'd make them watch me. It's me, Jordanna, and Sagit. So far we're calling ourselves either "Yer a Peein, not European" or "Yanic Sleuth," but we're gonna change it to something more artsy soon. We've written three songs already, and as soon as we learn how to play them, we're going to tour the world, or at least have a little party.

So far we've been mixing business and politics in other words we're hoping to incite worldwide revolution and maybe play some shows. We sound kind of experimental, kind of poppy and we all sing.

Yours for the revolution and the protection of all innocent bikes,

Elliot

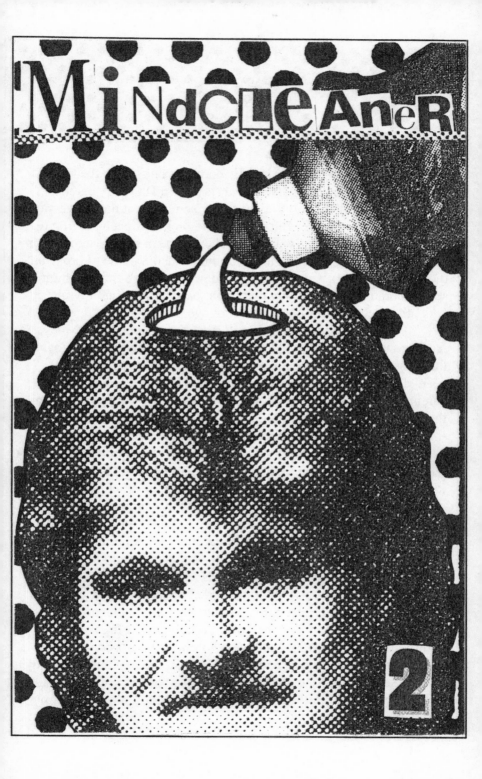

Welcome to Mindcleaner II: Zombie Punks from the Grave.

The good news (maybe): I'm staying in D.C. My parents offered (asked insistently) to finance my education at the University of Tennessee in Knoxville. But I'm not budging. It's been the first real break between me and my parents. They've been super parents all my life, from cleaning my skint knees to understanding when I broke all the windows of a hardware store. And now that I've finished high school and theoretically "sown my wild oats" and "found myself" in D.C., they're ready for me to go to college.

On the go-to-college-hand: The idea of spending my days reading, writing, and feeding my head seem infinitely more enjoyable than stocking organic raisins for 5 bucks an hour for another four years. Plus, it would make my nice parents happy. Plus the piece of parchment would help me get a job where I could work to change all the things that piss me off.

On the fuck-that-college-shit-hand: It's impossible to enjoy the things that I didn't earn. Buying records with parental cash doesn't feel as good as buying records with hard-earned cash. Even though it's the same record. (Not that I even really know what hard-earned cash is. Compared to so many... But the cash I earn is harder-earned than the cash that I've been given.)

College is another lap on the racetrack of American life, American Society. I could head for the finish line, but I know victory will feel hollow, because I started the race 100 yards ahead of everyone else. And it seems like my track is short and the obstacles few. I take a few steps from my parents' house to college and suddenly I'm declared a winner. Like waking up, going to the bathroom and taking a piss and the whole world starts cheering, shaking your hand, giving you 30,000 a year. No real hurdles, hunger, racism, sexism, war, etc. are in my way. And other people's tracks are miles long, full of bumps and cops. So I'm not too proud about my trip to the bathroom.

I could run, and pretend to care, but it's hard to even pretend to care when I already know that the race is rigged. I could just sit down and let the race go on all around me, but hey, I didn't rig the race, I want to have some fun, run somewhere. Unfortunately, it seems clear that the starting line isn't going to get evened out in my lifetime, and most days I don't feel like there's too much I can do to move any of the starting lines or to even-out the race.

But at least that feels like a challenge. Mostly, when my race is over, I want to feel proud, and like I earned some of the cheers. I don't want to wake up in twenty years feeling like a real winner for having taken a good piss. I want to still be angry about how rigged the race is. I want my blood to stay boiling.

So here it is, another issue of Mindcleaner, the school paper of Punk Rock Tech, a journal of people learning how to not run the race. Highly marketable skills include: Urban Communication (postering), Magazine Production and Layout (this is my term paper), and until recently, Advanced Budget Reduction (scams and shoplifting).

As usual, enjoy, and keep sending me letters...It makes me feel like I'm actually running some kind of "MAG" as opposed to just a zine, when I get to print your insightful commentary about the contents of this publication. Which reminds me- We finally got a letter that's printable, hope you enjoy it and learn from it as much as we did.

Yours for the disembowlment of hegemonic oppression,
Elliot Rosenberg, Editor in Chief
(in a non-hierarchical way, of course) (also known as "mama's boy")

Dear Mindcleaner,

I had the unfortunate experience of finding your so-called zine.

I say so-called because apparently no one ever told you that zine is short for magazine, which means that there's sposed to be stuff about records and punk rock music. What was that shit about going to visit your family? Who the fuck cares, you wussy mama's boy?

Here in N. Dakota that kind of shit is grounds for an ass-kicking. But since it was your 1st issue I'll forgive and use it for the lousy toilet paper that it is. Get it? I spose your pissed that I'm not going to recycle it. GET A LIFE.

John "Rock n Roll" Tucker

TOP TEN THINGS JOHN "ROCKNROLL" TUCKER AND I LIKE TO DO TOGETHER

1. Listen to Lenny Bruce Records.
2. Go to see Marchenko, live, for free at Fort Reno.
3. Watch *Life and Times of Harvey Milk*. It actually makes me nostalgic for the seventies.
4. Drink lemonade on the stoop when it's 105.
5. Read Mary McCarthy's *The Company She Keeps*. John and I often fight over who gets to be the widower of Mary McCarthy for the day. If only I were 60 years older and buried at her side.
6. Listen to KRS-ONE's speech at Georgetown.
7. Get letters. When John and I get letters, it gives each of us the feeling that although the world is incredibly fucked-up, that there are other people out there who are on our side and against all the bullshit.
8. Listen to Minutemen's "Double Nickels on the Dime."
9. Sit on the roof and watch night fall and listen to Patsy Cline. "Walking after midnight, searching for you."
10. Play basketball. The greatest American invention.

⭐ Remembering Facts

Read each sentence. Choose the correct answer and write its letter in the blank.

_____ 1. In Hawaii, Kenny Rogers owns (a) silk. (b) cotton. (c) denim. (d) flour sacks.

_____ 2. He was a good student until (a) 1977. (b) 1978. (c) 1979. (d) none of these answers

_____ 3. As a boy, Kenny once played and sang (a) water. (b) music. (c) culture. (d) none of these answers

_____ 4. He became the first Rogers to earn (a) wealth. (b) success. (c) milk cows. (d) none of these answers

_____ 5. When Rogers joined the New Christy Minstrels, he was how old? (a) 27 (b) 1978. (c) 1979. (d) 1980.

_____ 6. Kenny's third record label was (a) United Artists. (b) mineral. (c) United Artists. (d) happiness.

_____ 7. Kenny and Marianne wed in (a) 1976. (b) 1977. (c) 1978. (d) Columbia.

_____ 8. One song not a Kenny Rogers hit is (a) the drums. (b) the synthesizer. (c) keyboards. (d) the bass guitar.

_____ 9. The Knoll is a mansion in (a) 1962. (b) 1963. (c) 1964. (d) 1965.

_____ 10. Kenny Rogers considers himself a good businessman.

RIOT HERE RIOT NOW ON SEX WORK AND IGNORANT BOYS

The other day I was doing some thrift store shopping with a friend of mine who goes to college in Massachusetts and some boy who she brought along with her. (I guess that she was kissing him or something.) I didn't need any new clothes, but they were only intown for a couple of days and wanted to hit the big store in Laurel MD, so I went along for the ride.

While they were browsing through the swanky courdor oys and shoes, I wandered in to the dress aisle, and spotted this fine garment that I thouht might have to be mine. I found a corner with low traffic and finagled the dress on and my shorts and t-shirts off I went back to show my friend, and found her in the shirt aisles with her boy. "How does it look?" I asked.

"Pretty good...." the boy said, then added, "FOR WORKING THE STREETS IN!"

BULLSHIT ALERT!!!!

It works like this: Most of my friends work in the sex trade. Some of them take their clothes off for money. Some of them give "finger massages," for money. I think that a lot of people look down on women who choose to work in the sex industry, even supposedly open-minded punk rockers.

POINT ONE_ If anyone merits scorn it is the men who create the economic demand for these industries. most of these men hold places as respected members of the community, many with high prestige, high paying jobs. Women are denied access to many of these jobsand receive less wages for the

same work. WOMEN EARN SEVENTY THREE CENTS FOR EVERY
DOLLAR A MAN MAKES FOR THE SAME WORK. WOMEN OF
COLOR RECEIVE 59¢ FOR EVERY DOLLAR A MAN MAKES.

It is total bullshit that the men who create the
economic demand for these industries continue to
garner respect and xxxxxxx accolades while the
women who work in these industries are looked on
as trash, unfit for motherhood or wife.   Fathers
who have sex with prostitutes are rarely punished
and never declared unfit for fatherhood based on this
activity. (Oh, and by the way, women, how many
women do you know who get paid for being mothers and
housewives?)

Laws that penalize the women who sell access to
their bodies more than those that buy access to
those bodies are total bullshit. A society that
gives a knowing wink to bachelor parties while
giving a disgusted leer to topless dancers is full
of shit. Which brings us to-

POINT TWO- What a woman does with her body is
her business. If a woman chooses to respond to a
society stuffed with double standards by earning
her living exploiting men's fucked--up attitudes
about women, then RESPONSIBILITY (AND ANY BLAME
YOU WISH TO ASSIGN) BELONGS ON THE SHOULDERS OF THAT
SYSTEM, NOT ON THE WOMEN WHO HAVE TO DEAL WITH
THAT SYSTEM.

FUCK YOU to all men who want women
to take jobs at 73¢ on the dollar.
Who the fuck are you to judge?
SHUT UP AND
WORK FOR EQUALITY.
But definitely don't say shit in judgement.

P.S. Next time you stare at my breasts while I'm
talking to you , why don't you give me some money,

                                        jerk.

                -Christa

Making people understand

why I think that

COPS FUCKING SUCK

by Elliot

But wait, allow me to back up...
When I talk to the people who I've been friends
with since before I was a revolutionary punk
rock type guy, things always get uncomfortable
when anything that is remotely political (which is
just about everything) comes up. How can I
explain the political beliefs that I hold to be
true without spending five days recounting my
experiences and thoughts that have led me to
believe what I do. I don't have five days,
and usually the people listening don't have five
days.

Which means that up til now, I've blurted out
things that have made little sense, or have been

downright stupid. I mean, it is true that Cops
suck ass, but saying it like that doesn't change
many people's mind.. And if I leave a conversation
feeling further away from the person that I just
talked to then what's the point?

So I thought of a way to explain, in under five
minutes, why I think that Cops Suck. I putting
it in here so that you can use it if you find
yourself talking to people that love Cops and
law and order.

When I say that "cops suck," or "I don't think
there should be any cops," people always say
something like, "What are you saying, we should
just have total anarchy? What are you going to
do about the rapists and the killers. I think
that we need people around to protect us from
those who wish to do us harm."

So, my simple answer goes something like this,
"Cops don't protect us from those that wish to
do us harm. The job of cops is to enforce the
laws of the land. The laws of the land in this
country were written by slaveowners and the
descendants of slaveowners. The laws in this
country are mainly set up to protect property,

because they were written by people who have
the most property. So a cop's job is actually
to protect property more than to protect people.
I can prove this idea with this example: if a
person is starving and has no money, and he or
she goes into a grocery store that has an
abundance of food, and he or she steals some of
the food, it is a cop's job to arrest him or her.
If he or she tries to flee, it is a cop's right to
shoot. This has nothing to do with protecting
people. There are many other examples like this,
instances where cops act as the foot soldiers
for the rich.

Another thing about cops is that they very rarely
actually protect people. More often they try
to catch people who have already done something

that is against the law. If a person really
wants to end violence, then a good place to
start is by confronting violence. Vote
against more violent cops. Vote against
more violent weapons. Turn off the TV and
don't pay to see movies that are full of it.

But most of all, try to even out the balance of
power and wealth so that everyone has equal
access to things that they need to survive, that
way people won't need to take food, money,
property, power or life from other people.

And of course I can always bring up that having
police allows some fucked-up, bad individuals
more chances to do harm to other people as much as
it allows good people a chance to protect other
people.

Retro Takes It's Toll-Prom Comes Back In Style-No Lox, No Jocks, No Rocks (Off)
by Kate

This party was supposed to be like a punk prom or something... what a great idea, right? Wrong! Here's a recipe for fun: To make a Punk Rock Prom you take the most disappointing and awkward night of your life (prom) add a group of people who have banded together because they were unable to deal with high school (punks) mix together on low energy for a few hours and ...Voila! You get.... a really lame night, with a slightly better soundtrack than the first time around! Well, anyway, I decided, fuck it, I was gonna have fun. I found a great dress, gaudy, frilly, lame (that's la-may, not lame, you lame-o) and a hot date and I was ready to have some belly-laugh, falling-on-the-floor fun, for a change.

But even before the corsage had been pinned on my chest, things were already going wrong. My date had to cancel, something came up... He had to see a man about a horse who was having a bad hair day or something. But, I'm willing to give him the benefit of the doubt, so if he's reading and wants to ask me out again, well...

Though Oprah was calling me on the phone, begging me to be a part of the panel "How to Pick Up the Pieces, Shattered Prom Dreams," I wasn't ready to give into bitterness. Besides, I'm a feminist, I could go by myself.

The limo dropped me, things weren't too hoppin, but I bopped into the kitchen and got a beer, and set out to get the dance floor rockin. While I crafted my designs upon the dance floor, I munched on some chips and crackers. They were a bit dry: there was no pate at this partay. The only cheese around was found being squeezed from the speakers. But wait, this was a non-dairy affairy, Larry, and the tunes only appeared to be the real cheese of the Big Chill Soundtrack- it was actually the deeply soulful (tofu-based) alterna-oldies, that our parents certainly weren't hip enough to listen to back in the day.

I felt a little out of place, seeing as how everyone else was just dressed in the hipster-vintage-thrift-store clothes that they usually wear, only a little more dressy. But I guess I expected that, and whatever, I actually got some folks to dance with me.

So I get off the dance floor, and immediately so does everyone else (all three of them) and I can't find my beer. I was sure I had left it on the window sill by the couch, but oh well, I'll get another, no bother.

Head to the kitchen, it's pretty empty except for Eron McDunn, founder and still president of the Church of Straight Edge ("I like my mind just fine, I like seeing the world through unclouded eyes", -Small Menace '82) owner of Discontent Records. Eron is talking to someone next to the keg, for which there is miraculously no line. I sipped my crude cocktail, put the cup on the trusty window sill, and danced, pranced, romanced, took a chance. When I get done dancing I go for the beer, but hey, that's queer, I fear that the beer has disappeared. (I smell a beer thief. Actually, now that some of these punk kids have started dancing, that's not all I smell. At least at the original prom the kids wore deodorant.)

This is getting annoying, but I'm thirsty so I head back for another beer, and on the way I hear Eron say something like, "So then the guy from Ticketron says: who are you gonna cry to when you wanna play arena shows?" His conversation-mate gives a chuckle and they sip their tall glasses of tap water as I push by them and head out to the dance floor again. This continues and goes on like a bad T.V. sitcom or good avant garde theatre, and pretty soon I've nudged by Eron and friend about 1000 times to get a beer only to have it stolen by some hipster who is probably afraid that Discontent records won't put out their next single if Eron sees them drinking beer. I'm pretty sure he's not THAT judgmental or he probably would have stopped putting out records by people who try so hard to look like heroin addicts years ago. I mean GET REAL.

My beer drinking was put to an end when Eron's partner in conversation, on my final trip to the keg, asked: "Bad day at the office?" Ouch, there went my fantasies of a solo recording career on Discontent. Luckily, things finished on a good note, and I was elected prom queen and got a neat little crown. I'm not sure if I got votes because I was the only one to dress up and get down in the true spirit of prom, or if it was because I had inadvertently been the waitress for almost every person there who was desiring a beer. (Maybe it was all of those pieces of paper with my name on it that I stuffed into the shoe box.) Either way, I won, and to all of the rockers who voted for me - this Bud's for you.

#1 DUMB THING HEARD THIS WEEK

(Sorry to my anonymous friend
who will probably read this.)

1. "Capitalism makes me so sick. How much money Bill Cosby, Oprah Winfrey, and Michael Jordan make is disgusting." Please. Is it any coincidence that the three people you mention are all black, even though capitalism has clearly not led to black people having the majority of the wealth in our society. Do you really hate capitalism? Why? I thought it would be because of the people who really make the big bucks, not just the high paid entertainers, but the weapons producers, the clearcutters, the polluters. Or do you hate capitalism because three black people can make a lot of money by making beauty, making people laugh, entertaining people. (Also, I just read in the paper about Bill Cosby giving Spike Lee millions of dollars to finish production on a movie about Malcolm X that the studio had pulled the plug on.)

2. Almost as dumb as the fact that I heard this said and said nothing and backstabbingly write about it in this zine.

John's "gone west young man" and found fame and success!

GARLIC

For too long garlic has been known as the
    ketchup of the intellectual.
It's time to bring garlic to the people!
We can't continue to confine our garlic
        consumption to vegan potlucks and our
        own kitchens.
Now is the time to take to the streets and
        let everyone know:
Garlic is delicious: Add it to food, roast
        and spread it on bread, eat it raw.
Garlic is healthy: It wards off colds,
        high cholesterol, infections; it can be
        used to treat acne, it can be used to
        ward off vampires, politicians.
You can make soap out of garlic.
I like to rub it all over my lover's body
        and lick it off.
In the future cars will run on garlic,
        garlic will be used to generate
        electricity, to end war.
Garlic will save us all.
LEGALIZE GARLIC NOW!

-Jordana

Report from Agent 006.3

        Target: Q-Mart Mega Store
        Known information: open 24 hours a day.
0.25 miles side to side. Full grocery store
inside.
        Kind of establishment: THE ESTABLISHMENT.
The kind of place that makes assloads of money
gives noneof it to employees and drives small
businessess out of business,. Fuck them.
        Our mission: have fun, fuck with K-mart,
take no prisoners, be taked no prisoners.
        Description of activites: We arrived at
02:00 in a minivan, entered enemy territory an
d split into three units of two agents each. M
y unit made our way to the rear of the store,
the grocery department, where packages of
hamburger were sliced with razors and many
fruit was punctured to prevent its sale as a
profit making device for the enemy.

        Returning southwest, towards th front of
the store, we encountered unit two, who inform
ed us that they had performed operations of
sabotage in the candy and pet food aissles.
They reported that unit three was headed for t
he magazine area, to disarm many publications
that endeavored to promote the malnourishement
of women, that propagated the use of make-up.
Unit two headed off to the make-up aisle to
finish the rest of that work.

        My partner and I positioned ourselves
at the center of the store, where we could
stand lookout and assess the risk to various
stages of the operation. It just so happened
that we were in the shoe department. We
walked through the aisles, checking for shoes
that could be used in future missions.
Unfortuneately, a woman who believed to be
an enemy agent was busy stocking the shelves,
preventing us from acquiring any footwear, but

we were prepared to action in event of a diver
sion. Said diversion did occur, taking the form
of the sound of a 90 lbs bag of dog food falli
ng to the floor, then a second one, busting
open. The enemy communication system blared,
"Damage control, asile nine,"   Shortly,
we heard a commotion, and I went to investigat
e.   Several employees of the store were running toward the east, toward the petfood
department. One had amop raised over his head
as if a weapon. I could hear shouting in the
distance and I feared the worst. I saw a secur
ity guard run by. Several of the womend from
the checkout counters ran toward the action,
their register keys swinging around their neck
s.   The commincation system onee again alerte
d "Damage control, asisle nine." Then the
song private dancer, by Tina Turner began to
play. I ascertained that the dmage control un
it was dealing with x fellow employees
of the store (and not my comrades) and I retur
ned quickly to the shoe department. My partne
r and I made the most of the diversion,
replacing out own battered footwear with
the finest that the enemy could offer us.
Unfortuneately, ther wasn't much time to look
at sizes. I cut the shoestrings with a
razorblade, and headed for the door.

Unfortuneately, my run was slowed by
untied shoes, and the suspected enemy agent
from the next aisle was now hot on our heels,
yelling, "Hey where's your friend going with
my shoes?" My partner called to the agents
alerting them that it was time to abort.
I made it through the front door as the
sound of "Loss control, front gate, loss
control, front gate," began to bellow from
said enemy agents mouth.

A possible idisaster was averted by
the ingenuity of one of our agents who had
been to the hardware department and enlisted
the aid of one roll of enemy duct tape to cove

r our liscence plate with duct tape. Last out of the building was the agent with keys, and hot on her tail were three enemy agents with note pads for the purpose of writing down our plate numbers. But they were foiled, and the loss control officer was nowhere in sight, probably breaking up another altercatio n in the dog food aisle.

On the backroads toward home, we tallied our confiscations: a pack of licorice, a bag of popcorn, five glue sticks, a roll of duct tape, and a pair of white vinyl running shoes. There was initial dissappointment at the small ness of our profits, but we realized that the enemy casualties had been high, and all of our agents made it safely back to home base without any losses. I would deem this mission a success.

ROAD TRIP TO SEE THE NOT VENERATED ENOUGH WALLAHACKACAMA,
A.K.A. THE TWO MIRACLES OF THE CHURCH OF LATTERDAY PUNK ROCK
THE GOSPEL ACCORDING TO ELLIOT THE BAR MITZVAHED

February 14, the ballyhooed corporate day of love. We (Tomothy, Jordana and me) were being unpatriotic, failing to consume any schmaltzy love shit. But we did make a pilgrimage of love to see the Wallahackacama Sound Machine in Waterbury, Connecticut, so don't think that we weren't trying our damaged best to participate in the traditions of this fine country of ours, 'cause we were.

It began Friday night, after I closed at the Natural Food Co. When I drag--assed through the door of my sleepy house it was Jordana nd Tomothy brewing coffee and travel plans. Jordana said, "So are you with us or against us? I mean, its a rare Wallahackacama show."

"Vroom, vroom," said the vintage Chevette, and we were off. Loaded to the rear-view mirror with vegan treats courtesy of Natural Food Co.

Tomothy's collection of Wallahackacama's 7 inches playing on the back right speaker, the speaker that has refused to die. I awoke at 3:30 a.m. as we decelerated into the Walt Whitman Rest Stop on the Jersey Turnpike. "I sing the body electric."

We played some excellent Funhouse pinball.

I drank my coffee and was all geared up
for my stint behind the wheel, but the Chevette
That Could, well it wasn't up to the pressure
of a Valentine's Day affair. We tried all the
simple tricks to make the car work, felt
embarrassed by how little we understand the
machinery that we rely on everyday, then opted
to hang outoutside the food court and wait for
sunrise/ miracles.

And right on schedule, just as we were about
to call and purchase an AAA membership on Jordana's
parents' credit card- through the gates of
Walt Whitmanland rolled none other than the

vaunted Wallahackacama. We threw caution to the
wind, left the Chevette to fend for itself
against the demons of the Travel Oasis, and were

graciously accommodated on Roadvan Wallahackacama.
The quarters were cramped, but the company superb
(though mostly asleep) as we rolled through
picturesque highwayland to Waterbury.

The show started at 3 p.m. in the V.F.W. of
Waterbury. It was a benefit for Planned Parenthood
of Connecticut, and raised somewheres around $400
plus gas moeny for the bands. ASSASSINS OF BUSH
started things off with a roar and the tempo didn't
slow down as ANTILAW hurled themselves about in a
fit of feedback. Just when we thought that we woul
would all need to take a break for resuscitation in
the snow, WALLAHACKACAMA took the stage for 45
minutes of intense, politically-minded mayhem. If
you haven't seen them, they're well worth the drive
to Connecticut (or beyond)... Even if a Chevette
must be sacrificed to get there.

After a fine evening amongst newfound friends (vegan burritos as big as our heads) we caught a ride with some kids from Richmond, and it was Van Halen, Journey, and Chumbawamba all the way to the place that so honors Walt Whitman. In a daze from the road, heads still spinning from burritos and classic rock, we piled our bodies into the Chevetter as if it had never been broken. In the futile gesture of a sick joke, Tomothy put the key in the ignition, turned, and, like the hasty

end to a poorly plotted T.V. pilot with religious

overtones, the engine started and purred like a kitten. Ours was not to question why, ours was but to drive, drive, drive.

So that's it. If there is some sort of higher power, I suppose she/he/it wished to impress upon us the value if carpooling. And a lttle brother-sister love amongst the punks.

Thus spaketh the apostle Elliot, and on that ay he converted another twenty souls. Plus we still had some vegan treats to take us through the post Valentine's Day depression.

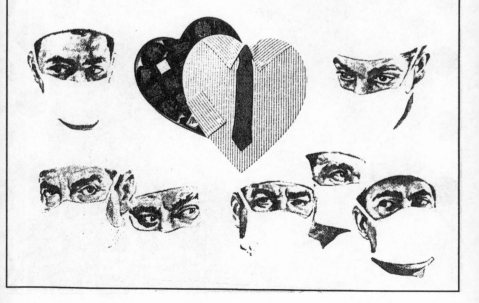

At this point I am trying to do the let's be friends dance with some degree of sincerity. Snotty. I mean I genuinely want to want to be friends, but mostly I feel angry and like I don't want to see her.

Her reply (of course) is that if I don't want to be friends then it proves that I was only in it for the sex (obviously untrue, sex was nonexistent, except for that one time, when it was bad). Mostly I was in it cause I thought you were rad, but then shit between us got so confused, so sex-interrupted-because-a-phone-call-was-more-important. I just wish that I had gotten with someone who liked sex, or liked me, or both.

We started out agreeing that we were gonna dance. But it's really hard to dance with you when your leg is tied to the post of some idea that I can't understand, and that one leg just won't move. I'm not a jerk, I'm just trying to help because you don't know how to dance and it was your idea, and I know that I'm conforming to hegemonic constructs of the history of dancing as a mating ritual, but I came all this way and I wanna have some fun, can't you just let me lead for one song? Or you lead us both? Never mind, if I tried to cut that rope, your dancing leg would only be free to give a swift kick to my shin.

We just weren't meant for each other. But you were the perfect girlfriend for my guilt.

———————

Good practice, finally. Made it all the way through 4 songs, pieces of three others. Hope we play a lot of shows before Sagit goes to college. First show- one week. Six whole songs?

Weird to be playing songs about destroying sub-urban America and then come upstairs and eat good vegan cookies fresh out of the oven.

Nightmare about getting busted shoplifting. I got my one phone call and I had to call home. Hannah had to accept the collect call, then put Mom on the phone. I had to explain that I was in jail, for shoplifting. There were pigeons flying around and I had to keep ducking, and people yelling in the background.

"No, Mom, I wasn't shoplifting, it was sabotage. Cutting profit margins and undermining class-stereotypes. Don't you see, Mom? Can't you see?"

Pigeon shit and that smell, and the yelling echoing like in a million empty high-school shower rooms.

"I just need bail, I can pay you back, it's just sabotage."

Happy to wake up.

First show. Super nervous onstage. When we started playing everything was cool. Before "Tension," I talked about the song being about the way that rock stars take up too much space. When I came out of the pay-attention-to-what-you-say-so-you-don't-fuck-up trance I found that I was staring at Aaron Pavapolous, Pretty Boy. For a second I was feeling guilty, but then he was so intently combing his hair that I don't think that he heard me. It was really fun being onstage. Eron said that he liked it, and I felt like Mean Joe Green had just thrown me the towel. His niceness, genuineness, never ceases to amaze me.

Last night I had a dream where I stormed into a high school where a congressman was speaking to a government class and I pulled a gun on him and made him explain why he had voted for all of this legislation that clearly made it harder for people to survive. I made him tell all of these kids why he wanted take away funding from education programs and pass a law that allowed 14 year-olds to be tried as adults and go to prison for life for selling drugs.

And today I got letters from two prisoners about bills going to the senate to make it harder for prisoners to file appeals and sue for abuse, torture or injury by guards.

Rock was really good today. Don't know what we'll do come September. New drummer? Close up shop? Worries for another day.

Jordana's new lyrics:

Something gets lost
In the translation
We act upon impulses
Described in our text books
Written by scholars
And sealed with a kiss
My mouth hurts your mouth hurts me
Your body and my eyes
Speak different languages
I lick my lips, you hold my tongue
You sealed my lips with a kiss
My mouth hurts your mouth hurts me

The prettiness of things that she writes, music and words. The first time she plays a song.

Oy yoy yoy. So now it's Marchenko, Colburn, and the Luminaries for the Food Not Bombs benefit.

And it's all my other friends in bands that are vaguely to explicitly pissed that I didn't ask them to play with Marchenko. But at least all the equipment and space and flyers and people to work the show are done. So I can sleep easier now, knowing that my only worries are the people who are pissed about not getting to play. But they'll have to come, because most can't even say it to my face, because it's a benefit, because Eron goes to every one of their shows and puts out all of their records.

Sept 23, 1992

Dear Maureen,

Hey rocker. What's happenin in O-hi-O? How's the roommate sitch?

Things are at the usual level of hectic here. New job, thanks to UMD's job search system. I work at this after-school program on Fourteenth Street, just a four block commute. I coordinate tutors and get parental permission slips and ask the principal for access to different rooms in the building. The idea is that children from the neighborhood, which is classified as "low income," stay after school for classes in art and music and two times a week have tutoring. My job is to find tutors for these kids. Most of the tutors come from the colleges, Howard and Georgetown being the most frequent contributors.

It's really nice to work with kids for a change. It's pathetically Catcher-in-the-Rye-esque, but children are so much easier to think only good things about. Especially when I live in the purgatory of punk rock. Actual kids instead of adults showing their solidarity with youth by acting like any sign of sophistication is "selling out…"

The scene is like this: tutors show up about 5 o'clock. They go look for the tutee, who usually is there and psyched. (I don't know why, but for me to paint this picture I need to say that all of the students are Black or Latino.) Tutors come from two main groups, college students (mostly black, but some white and Latino) and private sector do-gooders volunteering on their way home from work (almost all white). Most of the college kids (though not all) seem to see (interact with?) the kids as kids, which makes the program seem cool and good for the kids- an adult who dependably comes and hangs out and reinforces the idea that learning is important...

But a lot of the private sector do-gooders seem to see the kids a part of some statistic about our society and do things like have the kids repeat "I will not drop out of school," five times at the beginning and end of each session. Which is all about some fucked-up biases which ain't cool for the kids to interact with...

Whatever, at least they give a shit, even on some fucked-up level, about stuff that's going on in the city. The suburbs usually are just a way of putting the city out of sight, out of mind, and out of tax-base, even as they continue to use city services and depend financially on income earned in the city.

Hmmm. I guess I needed to say some stuff. It's strange to be on the other side of the school desk. Mr. Rosenberg...

(unfinished and unsent) -ed.

Sitting around the Nest after the meeting shooting the shit and cleaning. Aaron Pavapolis came in to see if we had any issues of *Cometbus*. Weird watching the politicos. Everyone very aware of his presence. He was just coming in for a zine, which happens all day long, but everyone was hanging on his every movement, trying to seem like they weren't paying any attention to him. We were all paying attention, some admiring, some waiting for ammunition for gossip and mockery.

I showed him *Cometbus* and rang him up, and he said "Thanks. Things going well here?" I was totally flustered and self-conscious, couldn't decide if I should be curt and just say "yep," or if I should tell him random details about living there and running the store. Afraid if I said too much it would look like I gave a shit about him because he's famous. (Always forgetting that acting normally, if the person weren't famous, equals acting friendly.) I guess my discomfort was obvious, he stopped talking abruptly and took off. Or maybe that's just how he is. Hard to tell in this scene when people are acting like jerks because they are jerks, and when they just don't know how to act, cuz they were all social outcasts in high school.

It's weird being part of a community built around ideas like rejecting fame, and yet most of the people involved are famous on some level. No one wants to be a jerk, but after a while I guess you can't tell whose being sincere. Plus if you play with a band, you end up knowing so many people in such minor ways, but I guess it seems like a responsibility to act friendly so you don't seem like an aloof famous person. But then no one knows if you're being sincere.

Drummer issue is settled. Hope Tomothy and I can live and rock together.

September 28, 1992

Elliot,

I have no idea how to begin this letter. I feel bad for writing to you about all of these things that are

on my mind, I feel like I should call you. But I needed to write and rewrite these thoughts so I could
make them as clear as possible. I am writing to you
about breaking up. I know that we aren't really
going out, and haven't been for some time, but I
still feel like I need to break up with you.

I don't know how you dated someone last year.
Not in the "how could you?" way, but in the way
that I know that I was the closest person to your
heart, and it's bizarre and fracturing to be physical
with someone other than the person that you are
closest to.

It's strange to ask for space when we're a thousand miles apart, but right now you live in the deep-
est recesses of my brain. I smile when I hear jokes
that would make you laugh, hold conversations
with you in my head. Sometimes I wish that you
could see the images in my head, that you lived with
a phone by your head so I could tell the story of the
latest ridiculous thing that I heard in class.

You know all this. I think that because we never
broke up, parts of my head and heart think that we
are still dating. When I meet people who I might
want to date, I think about how you would think
about them, which makes the idea of dating someone else seem crazy. I need more distance. I need to
stop writing you all my thoughts and start telling
them to people near me. I need to stop waiting to
tell you all my stories. I need us to break up, for
reals.

As I finish this letter I feel numb. I wait for the
weight of this letter to come around a thousand
different corners, bumping casually, politely into
me. It just happened, as I was writing. My mother
called and asked about Thanksgiving plans, if you
were coming home at the same time.

It's ugly that there are three other drafts of this

letter. I feel like a conspirator against life, plotting this death. Shifting words around, making paragraphs to make the ideas segue "naturally" into one another.

That brings me to the end. I love you. I know that we will be friends after some time. Right now, though, I need and love you as more than a friend, and since you can't be that, I need to learn to live without the crutch of our friendship.

I hope that I haven't caught you too off-guard. If you need to talk, you can call.

I love you.

Maureen

I wish I was living at my parents' house. Or a hotel or something. Somewhere clean and quiet. Watch tv and cry or have a fit or something. Something.

No more conversations. "That record label is getting distributed by Caroline, and you know they're owned by Geffen." "Is that made with sodium lactylate?"

"Bullshit about bullshit and that band and my food bullshit." Shut the fuck up.

Every friend of Christa's reminds me of what Maureen said about being physical with someone other than the person you feel closest to. Also how Maureen was my safety net, because I think everyone here is talking about me behind my back. Makes sense, since they all talk about everyone else behind their backs. It was nice to have one person who I know Christa hasn't told about how "manipulative" our relationship was.

It's a sure bet you're depressed when the only thing that you want is for time to pass quickly. I want to call Maureen, but also want to give her the space she needs, so that we can be friends again.

The sooner the not-friends part starts, the sooner it will end, the thinking goes.

It's anti-beauty, that time assuages all pain. That eventually this won't hurt. That at some point in the future I'll walk down the street, see a couple, and not think of her.

But at least it's something to look forward to.

Favorite band ever. The whole show I'm thinking Maureen, money, door, Maureen, equipment, no kids passing out in the bathrooms, security deposit. And only Jordana and T. K. helped sweep.

Marchenko plays pretty much every song that I would put in the movie soundtrack of my life, but I have to make sure people don't stage dive and there's enough change at the door. But we made $435.

Bands playing downstairs. Need to read. Need to sleep. Need to not be groggy at work tomorrow. Helpless feeling - not being able to control the noise in your own house. Punk is punk, but I want a house. Punk sucks.

If I had to live here, have this lifestyle, put up with everything, and my days were mostly taken up by something like helping people find the best organic colon cleanser, I'd be gone. At least my new job doesn't suck.

Already catching shit from Tomothy about trying to dress up for work. "Dude, how can you partici-pate in a system where you have to wear a uniform?"

Tomothy, destroying the hegemony with his torn jeans at Atomic Records in Georgetown. There he goes, fucking up The Man- that's not a Time

Warner product- it's a record by a small-time capitalist who only wants to be big-time.

Hollow. It's all hollow. Hollow. Hello, I'm Hollow. Hello Hollow. Hollow. How low.

Everything else was stolen, so we took a look,
I am just the newest in a long line of crooks.
I'm a good student, I learn my lessons well:
If I can use it, then it must be mine to sell.
"The newest in new" the freshest fruit in the
    basket.
But the ladder that we're climbing
Is fashioned from caskets.
You're so cold, "The newest in new"
To be so cold is what history taught you
Taught me too.

Maybe. Maybe too preachy.

Tense practice. Ready to kill someone. Tomothy is becoming a prime candidate. But we all play really hard and after it's over I feel like I've sweated out some of my frustrations. Still feel like shit. Being in a rock band with people is not as good as being in love with them.

Want to call Maureen.

Showdown at the VFW Corral

Like a high school battle of the bands, it seemed, or prom maybe:

Our side, the Politicos, was out for Antilaw, but the Mt. Pleasant Fashion Posse had shown up in full force to cheer for turncoat faves Intergalactic Chaos Conspiracy. In the past, there been a tacit agreement due to a shared common enemy, but when Ill at Ease cut a deal with Warner/4AD, the in-fighting began. Tomothy fired the first salvo for our side, hanging up a poster of a big UPC bar code, with the words "Ill at Ease" where the numbers should be, in our clubhouse.

As the inevitable confrontation loomed, I looked around me and thought how small the whole thing was. Most outsiders wouldn't be able to tell us apart. The same wallet chains, retro clothes from the same decade. Just a difference in opinions about music's role in politics. That moment of clarity should have told me that it would be me who would have to represent for our side. And small though it may be, no punk goes against his clique. When my challenger came my way, I was not going to back down.

"I'm Mac, from Ill at Ease."

"Hi" I gave him a tough look.

"You got a problem with my band?"

I waited, weapons ready.

"I heard about the poster. Real cool."

"We thought so."

"Yeah?"

"Yeah. And we made it ourselves, we didn't even have to pay child laborers in Thailand 12 cents an hour."

"So that's the way it is?"

"Yep. We're not going to carry your record."

Sexy and violent, huh?

Whatever... When you sell over 100,000 records, you're "established." Ripe for the making fun of. Punk has always been about calling bullshit, so if you want to hang around punks, get used to being called on your bullshit. Just because you used to put out your own records doesn't mean you can do whatever the hell you want now.

God, our roles get dull. Can't believe other people aren't tired of playing them too.

All the politicos were here getting ready for the rally. Wish they had more of a sense of humor. Feel like a flake for not going to all of the meetings. I think what they're doing is important, but lately I just feel overwhelmed with boredom by all of this. I don't want to be disruptive, or counterproductive or whatever, so I guess I should steer clear. I don't want to be apathetic, but I'm dying from boredom.

Like they're doctors standing over the patient of American society, which is cool, but it's not like if somebody makes a joke or takes a break to drink a beer that the patient will die on the table. It's already dead. Why let it kill us all the time?

Except for Matt and T.K. who, by reading Emma Goldman and Hakim Bey, have realized that the patient must experience joy and humor. Once you've decided that joy and humor are part of the revolution and that you need to live the revolution, then even having fun is so important that you can't screw it up.

"Damn it, don't get analytical, we're in the moment. This is our fun time."

Tina's such a flake. Ignore me after we lived in the same house for six months. "We're in high school again." Wonder what article of clothing wasn't punk enough. Fuck this. Fuck this.

Despite everything else, me and Tomothy are good in a band together.

It seems like the guys in Colburn don't have much in common, but they are united by rock, or at least the desire to be on stage together. Like those married couples who don't talk, but then act all lovey-dovey when company is over. Making love to the audience each, not really into each other.

It's strange that I think of Colburn as a big band, out of our league, but there were only about 40 people to see them in New York. Still, it's weird to come to a town where you don't live and have 40 people you don't know want to come see you play and buy your records.

There was a dude with a kippah at the show.

the pessimist club

☺God has given you only one face, and you make yourselves another.☺

☺Cleverness is serviceable for everything, sufficient for nothing.☺

☺Every word you read changes the shape of your brain.☺

☺Gender colors the way you see everything. Don't try to deny it.☺

☺You are not as cool as you would like to be.☺

☺Run far away.☺

becca and i caught up with **the pessimist club** after their show at abc no rio. gear safely stowed, we headed out for chinese food, and then green tea, green tea- jittery me. the tea loosened their tongues and jordana(bass, vocals, good with chopsticks), elliot(guitar, vocals, fair with chopsticks), and tomothy (drums, skillful with chopsticks) gave us the goods.

elliot and jordana have been playing together for about a year. their original drummer moved to michigan, and tomothy has been playing with them for about 3 months.

live, jordana and elliot alternate introducing songs, which ususally have pretty political lyrics. high energy and emotive rock n roll.

irene: so you guys are a dc band?
elliot: we're from dc.
irene: do you consider yourselves part of the dc scene, discontent records, all of that?
tomothy: i guess so.
elliot: well, we try to play shows in dc. our record isn't going to be on discontent, but they're cool about helping us get out-of town shows. and they're super cool in general.
irene: so, what's up with the riot grrrl thing? are you considered a riot grrrl band?
jordana: i don't really know what that means. i mean, riot grrrl was a really important thing to me- relating the ideas of feminism to my life. i might call myself a riot

grrrl, but I don't want to be labeled by what other people think that means.
to me it has to do with confronting sexism in the punk scene and everywhere else, it's not just like some kind of music or a group of bands. yes i'm a riot grrrl, period. this is our band. with three people.

becca: do you think there's a trend for younger bands to defy labels more and be more political, like with riot grrrl and nation of ulysses?

tomothy: being in a band isn't really political

jordana: a lot of bands just use a lot of words like "revolution" or "uprising" or sing about political things, but most of them don't really take it beyond singing about it.

irene: so how do you guys take it beyond singing about it?

elliot: the thing is, a lot of bands sing about revolution, but it's just for show.

irene: but you guys have the guns? you're ready to kill cops and riot in the streets?

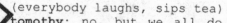

(everybody laughs, sips tea)

tomothy: no, but we all do activism that goes beyond selling records or small-scale capitalism. we're not playing like we're revolutionaries just to fill some niche in the music market.

elliot: and we're not equating ourselves with the black panther party, while providing none of the services, like literature or free breakfast or protection from cops. when a band like nation of ulysses sings about revolution one month, and then they're singing about grape juice and planet of the apes the next month, it just seems like they're making fun of people who really are oppressed and see revolution as a real answer

to their problems. or like it was
fashionable last month, but now it's "so
'91."

becca: your lyrics are pretty political...
how do you write songs?

jordana: well, elliot or i usually write
stuff, and then bring it to practice, and
then we all talk about it.

elliot: it might start with words, or it
might start with the music...

jordana: and we sometimes add to or change
what the other person has done. and tomothy
looks over the lyrics.

tomothy: they don't let me say anything.
actually i just hate writing stuff and i
can't sing and play drums.

irene: it seems like you put a lot
of emphasis on the words in your
songs.

elliot: well, it's like if you play
in a band, eventually you're going to
play in front of other people... and
if you don't have anything to say...

jordana: especially at shows. it's
a real chance to communicate.

tomothy: getting free food is cool
too.

(some of the interview got lost here,
because I didn't flip the tape,
ooops)

becca: what are your plans for the future?

tomothy: more interviews, more free chinese
food.

jordana: revolution, win **elliot:** sexist pig.
the lottery, get some (noogie fest erupts)
action

look for a pessimist club 10" out on 33rd revolution
records in the spring.

We've survived our first mini-tour. I think we still like each other.

Kids from Tri-State Transmitter took us to a cool diner. Seem like fashion punks, but walk the walk. Tomothy got to network. Me and Jordana got onion rings. He told them they'd be better off playing at the Nest than El Pollo, hope I don't have to set up the show. Seems like Tomo probably will, if he doesn't flake out.

A cool thing about Tomothy is that even though he gets pissed everytime he reads the paper, and is always outraged at the system, when I tell him that I'm moving out of the Nest, he says, "Cool. Where are you moving to?" Maybe all his anger is suppressed, but we get along.

Hornets
Nest

House
Journal

Keeping minutes are The Man, but we still want to record this stuff (for us and other groups to learn what to do and not to do...) We enter exhibit R in the ongoing struggle: Hornets Nest Collective Book number 2.

Please Leave Comments, suggestions, ideas, requests, jokes, band recommendations, questions and personal ads.

Can you guys order the Wallahackacama Sound Machine "Destroy Malignant Manifestation" 7" on Exhume records?

Thanks for letting us spend the night. Thanks for the grub... You guys gotta do something about those rats, they're gonna take over the whole building soon.

-Actomatics

Hey is it okay if Wigwam Warriors play here on December 7th? They called and asked for a show (gas money donation)?

-Jessica

I'm sick of bands playing here, it would be nice if some more people would help clean up afterwards, or maybe clear it with all the people who live here. Are Wigwam Warriors all boys? I'm sick of boy bands. Also- what's up with that name?

-Rebecca

Look, we accept pretty much every non-offensive band that we can accommodate. We didn't choose for them to be all boys.

-Tomothy

Who blamed you? What's up with being defensive, white boy?

-Paula and Marian

Whatever, quit bitching, start your own group. DIY means Y and not W for whining.

-Another White Boy

Fuck you, pig. Thanks for trying (for the millionth time in our lives) to silence our voices. Just because you admit that you're a white boy doesn't mean that you have to act like one.

-Paula and Marian

ACT-UP'S DIE-IN ON THE CAPITOL ON FRIDAY! BRING A TOMBSTONE.

Boy this is a discussion that will enlighten and edify all who read. I'm so glad that it's recorded... Good food, good meat substitute. That I'm thankful I can not refute. Thanks for the hospitality and floor space (some of the most comfortable concrete I've ever slept upon)

-Attica 4

What's up with kids coming to the store being so rude to the neighbors? Maybe we should put up signs that say something like, "Don't be a dick to our neighbors."

-Elliot

What do you mean "being rude?" Can you give an example?

-Jessica

When we had that 25Bonker show last week, some man was trying to ask for directions to the metro, and the kids here would not even tell him. When he came in, everyone is acting tense and quiet, like they thought he would rob us with arms. Perhaps we should have some workshops on racism.

-Inga

I don't think that workshops would really do anything, since the white hardcore kids from the suburbs will only come here to see bands and buy records/zines. But still we need to say something at every show.

-Matt

What can we say? I feel like the issue is more complicated than just people being rude. We live in a store, it's open to the public, and we can't really control who comes in, and as long as we are affiliated with punk stuff, it's going to be mostly white kids with money from the burbs, not anyone from this neighborhood. Our presence (as white, young folks with cash) is already detrimental to this neighborhood being for the people who are already here. We make other whites feel comfortable moving here, helping to raise rent, we support businesses which cater to our culture (the natural foods store) and the whites who move in on our cue are not going to have a problem calling the cops to protect their property, in fact we might not have a problem with that...

-Elliot

What are you advocating, segregation? If Black people were moving into an all white neighborhood in the suburbs, you'd be all for it.

-Frank

We could try to sell more soul and rap records to appeal more to the people who already live in the area.

-Tomothy

GENERAL NEST MEETING NEXT WEDNESDAY, 8PM COME EARLY TO WRITE LETTERS ON BEHALF OF DEATH ROW PRISONERS

Hey, thanks for letting us stay here. Thought we'd put in our two cents: Why don't you guys spend your money renting a place that doesn't have rats? This joint is a dump! Is it that important for you to live in this neighborhood? Fuck being rude, you guys are getting ripped off. For less money you can get a bigger and better space, and not be "ruining" the neighborhood, except in the ways that the burbs need to be ruined. Also, Wigwam Warriors are all boys. They sound like the Smiths trying to be spirit of '76 , which is unpleasant.

-Guys from Chicago

Yeah, but I thought we came to save the masses from poverty and despair through revolution.

-Anonymous Smartass

Hey, what do you guys think about having a separate book

for people who live here and are part of the collective and another book for people passing through? It seems like we need to be able to talk about stuff without hearing about the rats and whatever else.

-Tomothy

Hmmmm... and we thought that you guys were going for inclusiveness... Oh well, it isn't the first time that white men have lied about their intentions... Seems like you're trying to shut our voices up, especially since we say what all the grrrls in this collective think, but know that they have to share space with you.

-Paula and Marian

Accidentally stole this book. Oh, well. Property is theft right?

A new writing journal, with a preface about why I must exile myself from the world of the collective punkrock book & record store/ house/ soapbox. Sometimes I want to say "Shhh, don't interupt," but how we decide is at least as important (in this project) as what we decide. Question is how to deal with that interruption, without making people feel inferior or silenced, and still get things done, not be hijacked by the insane making irrelevant points with the fervor of preachers.

In the end, our presence is more disruptive than productive (or maybe unnoticed) for people who live here, even if we have managed to sell a few copies of *Blood In My Eye* at low cost.

Paula disagrees: "We're not gentrifiers, we're strippers."

"G Force"
When the spaceship landed
The aliens said, "Be cool
We haven't come to colonize you,
We've come to build a movement.
We were chased from our homes by
    businessmen
We had to get out, get out or go to
    school."
Pretty soon the aliens' cousins arrived
    and said, "Hey, we like this food!"
Then the shopping malls appeared.
The aliens, they vanished, without col-
    lecting their security deposits
But their cousins stuck around and ate
"authentic" food.

Tomorrow Jordana, Kate, Sam and I sign the lease on a house in Mount Pleasant. It's already gentrified there. So me and my status quoian self can feel all safe.

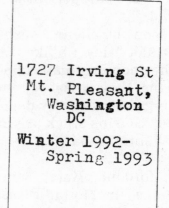

1727 Irving St
Mt. Pleasant,
Washington
DC

Winter 1992-
Spring 1993

New house. Big, hardwood floors, attic, basement for practice, no rats.

Still depressed. New house is better and all, but not the all better that I was hoping for. Wish that there were magic words that would make everything pretty. Or at least a plan that I was a part of that had a chance of making everything right:

First we'll take the television stations, just one. Cable. We won't even broadcast views, just random shots, twenty seconds of footage from every life in America. The rich houses, the shitty jobs, the boring minutes of school, the rotting garbage in poor parts of town, the sad people in ugly places, the sad people in glitzy places, homeless people, twenty seconds of two million people in jail, twenty seconds of people at work making things uglier.

Yeah, and then everyone will rise with millions of voices, take to the streets, demanding that good things happen and bad things stop. And they'll all be grateful that we took over ESPN to show the images. And we'll be revolutionary heroes.

Ah, there are so many ways to really make the world pretty. I mean in this democracy, land of the free, surely, it's gonna change soon. I could just run for president and then probably win, and then I can make it right. Oh, or a really good record that says what I'm thinking. If I just tell everyone about the fucked-up things I see, then everyone will care and want to change things. If I just yell real loud that the schools that my students go to suck, that they're falling down and full of shitty teachers who don't care, then when people hear, they'll drop what they're doing and get right to work to make things good and fair for all kids.

Colin and Nora on the way back from a Baltimore wedding. (Of people my age!) They're staying with Nora's friend. Nora seems nice and smart although we don't have much in common. I guess that Colin and I only have Wilson in common. She's doing a paper on U. S. Mexican relations and the sex-trade and wanted to check out an American strip bar. She hadn't been and thought that she needed to for the paper. (Neither had I. Colin didn't say if he had or not.) Stupidly I mentioned King's Castle, and then we were going. Colin and I walked, but Nora was late. Started to rain, we went inside.

Saw Angie on stage inside, and waved to her. (What's a "feminist" boy to do in this situation? Which kind of wave? A "Hey, how's it going," while her legs are spread wide with some guys face inches from...) We sat down. Total freak-out mode. Watched a hockey game I didn't care about on a TV behind the bar.

Two stages, and women who'd just finished dancing were walking around saying, "Thanks for watching." The women on both stages were naked except for their shoes and a garter, with their legs spread apart. Each one had a thirty year-old man's nose about two inches from her vagina. The men would look for about 30 seconds, then insert a bill in the garter.

Couldn't deal. We went outside to wait in the rain. When Nora got there we went to Burrito Bros, then headed to Dupont Circle. Told them I didn't want to go back, but didn't care if they went. And then they did. And then I walked home. The end.

A real man now.

The best answering machine message ever:
Tim Chrompson (not just a rock star, but also our

next door neighbor) in the voice of the Godfather: "You guys should be extremely careful who you talk shit about."

Guess Tri-State Transmitter wants to play El Pollo Negro.

"I heard that Sam told Tomothy that Muffy said that he wasn't going to be able to repeat what Biff had told Jim about the way that Jeff tells all of Jane's secrets to Jon. Sam's such a fuck. Oh, hi Sam, it's soooo nice to see you. BF4ever."

Don't want to practice today. The thing about music is that even if you say something really cool in a song, people can just listen to the music, they don't have to pay attention to the words. I don't want to waste all my good poems on a band that gets caught up in this shit.

———————

Dear New Yorker,

Please find enclosed two poems by the GREAT- · EST UNPUBLISHED WRITER IN AMERICA (me). I offer them first to you (You once published a poem by my great grandfather (Abe Issacson)).

They cost $1000 per poem, or $1800 for both (special discount because they're going to be published in New York, where so many Jews live).

Sincerely,

Elliot Rosenberg
1727 Irving St. NW
Washington, DC 20010

P.S. Don't try and shortchange me. You're dealing with a professional and I know what this stuff is worth.

———————

Jordana, Kate and Sam-

In case you don't remember me, my name is Angie and we met at a potluck at the Newton house in August. I brought potato salad in a big blue bowl and we talked about the bowl for a while.

I'm writing because I wanted to let you know that your housemate Elliot and his goateed friend came into the King's Castle yesterday while I was working. When I saw him from the stage I vowed that if I ever ran into him again I would kick his white-boy ass.

He and his friend walked in, ordered a coke and left without tipping.

I guess what really pisses me off about this is that Elliot thinks that he's so down with the strippers that he can bring outsiders into the Castle and parade the strippers around like he's a tour guide in some smutty zoo. One of the things that we were all working for and something that Elliot claimed to be working for in *Mindcleaner* is a place where women and strippers feel safe. I used to feel safe in the punk community, but it seems like now all the boys who say that they're into not viewing women as objects can flaunt their "accepted by and allied with strippers" position to the outside world and get to use our bodies as background scenery. Without tipping!!! I feel super pissed that somebody in the "community" (a HORNET!) would bring his friends in to look at me like a piece of meat. Elliot can't keep this a secret any more. He's more horn-y than horn-et.

If it had been just Elliot I would have handled it myself, but since the issues are different, maybe you'll want to confront him. At least I thought you should be warned.

Get back to me about this

Angie 265-1583

Feel like every time I deal with a punk rocker in this town they see me as a dirty old man who went to a strip club. I could be paranoid, it's hard to tell, people's social skills are so poor I can't tell if they're treating me differently. Cool that doing one thing that gets misunderstood can ruin your rep as a politically down punk rocker. Like they've seen the true me through this incident, and indeed, grrrls and boys, he is a pig. Waiting for the zine *Dead Elliots Don't Rape* to hit newsstands nationwide.

Sam's a little peeved to be losing punk rock points by living with such an out-of-fashion housemate. They had a three hour meeting with Angie. I think everyone is just embarrassed. Me most of all.

---

1. Write thank-you note to Discontent for list of venues and promoters. (Let them know that places in Louisville are closed.)

2. Call Brian about cover art. Recycled paper? Lyric sheet.

3. Send tapes to: Hannah, Maureen, Hattiesburg, radio station in Eugene

Christa wants me to help her move. Oy, yoy, yoy.

Amazing how Americans remember those that they've worked so hard to forget the rest of the year.

Santa, sitting stoically atop the housing project, chin resting on his fist as he looks down at the police handing out toys on the corner. His face is still, worn, but proud. This was the year that

Christmas almost didn't happen for everyone. There were a lot of children whose parents were jobless, many homeless. And through the efforts of various community organizations, under the supervision of Santa, or the collective goodwill of the citizens of Washington DC (whichever you believe in) Christmas did come this year. Every child got the things that he or she needed to make them feel loved: Batman karaoke machines, plastic photon guns that make realistic kill noises, new Nintendo cartridges, Barbies that talk when you pull the string in her back.

Cut to a shot of the moon outside, a silhouette of a sled, loaded with toys, pulled by reindeer, glides by.

A little salve on the conscience. We've conspired to give you shitty schools, an occupying army called the police to contain you, unhealthy living conditions followed by piss-poor medical care... But no kid should be without 47 Nintendo cartridges on Christmas.

Scientific research has found that hearts nourished on plastic can cause abnormalities in the growth of the soul later in life. This can lead to conditions which often result in such "anti-social behavior" as to merit lockdown.

Got Christa's column today. Saw her at Pollo last week. I was just telling Sam about dealing with some crap at work, and she was taking pity on me and rubbing my shoulders. Christa came over, and it was just insanely uncomfortable. It's been a long 10 months of trying to be friends. I think she just wants to be my friend because I put up with the trauma of it all. I don't want to be a jerk, but I can't coach her through another crisis with her housemates when I know that there'll just be another one next week, and I don't like her housemates anyway. Christa wanted to talk to me alone. We went downstairs by the bathrooms, and I was ready for her to grill me about the King's Castle incident, but she started asking me all these questions about Sam and whether we were involved. I convinced her that we aren't, even though it shouldn't matter at all to her at this point. Then she started telling me about some new drama with her housemates and tears were welling up in her eyes.

Not sure if I said this or just thought it, but it was something like, "Get a grip on your own life before you fuck with mine." I keep telling myself it's the best thing for her, but I still feel like a jerk. Sad.

Then she gives me this column about what a jerk I've been to her. (can she read my mind?) Basically, I'll be using Christa's pain to make my zine better, which makes me as big a prick as she says, but if I don't print it, it seems like I'm trying to hide what she has to say to save myself. She's a fucking genius.

Walking with Kate to get Ethiopian food, ran into Tina and walked together towards Adams Morgan. Outside Bubblez Laundromat, one of the guys who's usually drunk on the corner was on the ground, getting cuffed by eight cops. Kate and I stopped to witness. They were screaming at the guy, who was nose down to the cement, "Get up! Get on your feet, you slob!"

After about 15 seconds, Tina asked, "Why are you guys watching this? You can see this stuff on TV every night." 11 months after Rodney King, she wants to know why.

Kate and I stood there until he was hustled into a

patrol car.

Good meal. Good conversation. Still didn't sit well. Hard to enjoy food after watching the cops kick someone. Does it make me better than rest of America, who actively don't care, if it ruins my digestion for a while? Kate said about her job and it seemed even truer after what we saw, "People act a little better if they think that other people are watching them." What if they figure out that we'll watch forever (to salve our conscience) and never do anything (don't want to get hurt ourselves). What if we only watch?

January 25

Hannah,

I have been meaning to write for some time etcetera etcetera, but etcetera etcetera. And now, after months of silence, I am going to lean on you and ask you to see my Snuffalufaguses. Maureen was here visiting, and she's usually so good about seeing them, but Snuffs kept visiting during the stray minutes that she was preparing the letter of the day or counseling Oscar, or doing her hair, or something. So I turn to you, with hopes that if I've got to wear this heavy, feather-covered costume, you'll see that I'm not just imagining the hairy elephant.

Maureen and Sam and I had tickets to the Holocaust Museum for 11:30 and we went to Hellers Bakery on the way downtown. It was 10:30, so the punk rock breakfast rush was in full swing. A crowd of punk rockers was harassing the counter help with intricate questions about what kinds of margarine and wheat were used to make all of the baked goods. Sam and I introduced Maureen all around and people were surprisingly friendly and cheery. Maureen and Sam left to buy orange juice. The non-punkers who had been waiting while the P.R. kids got their vegan fix got served and left. One of the aproned employees came from the kitchen with a steaming fresh tray of poppy seed humentashen, so I ordered six (had to complete the authentic Jewish experience for Sam and Maureen). You'd have thought that I had sold my only begotten sister to the pharaoh or something. The punk rock peanut gallery: "You're eating that, that's made with butter," "Ewww, gross." I thought about throwing the Jewish issue/holocaust trip back in their faces, seeing how quickly I could hush them by bringing my oppression into play, but opted for the classy move, and walked them to the sidewalk where I threw the humentashen at them and ran to meet Maureen and Sam. (One busted Aaron Pavapolis's carefully sculpted coiffure.) Maureen and Sam asked for the baked goods, and I tried to explain what happened, but they just wrote it off as some joke of mine. (It's not so different than a lot of jokes I make.) Bad mood about the stupidity of the life I live here in DC for the length of the bus ride.

After pouting all the way to our stop, I remembered that Maureen was in town, which is all too rare, and found a good mood. We bought cornbread on the street outside the Smithsonian, and passed through the archway of the museum.

Oy yoy yoy, thirty billion displays of atrocities, people with our last name, someone with your exact name, Hannah Rosenberg. There was this guy who died in the Warsaw Ghetto Uprisiong that looked just like me. It was genuinely eerie. They all physically resemble us. And it was really obvious that anybody remotely political, who cared or protested, was going to end up super dead. And it was sad, but then I started noticing how there were pretty much only Jews being discussed and remembered how Dad had taken great pains to explain to me about gypsies and gays and Catholics being targets for extermination. And so I started paying attention and getting mad at the museum for excluding everyone else, but wait, then I found two mentions of gays and three of Catholics and two of Gypsies. And I started reading more carefully and so much of the text was about what great Germans the Jews had been and how they were so smart and what a tragedy it had been because of all the great brains and businessmen and poets that had died. The tragedy wasn't that millions of people were murdered, just that a lot of them were really smart. And I couldn't hold it all, all the evilness of the nazis and how sinister it was that the museum people had forgotten, excluded everyone else, and how the tragedy was that they were such great Germans.

I went and sat in the meditation room, which is conveniently shaped like a Star of David to mourn all the dead Jews. Sam and Maureen finished and found me there, and we started to walk out. They wanted to go to the bathroom before the bus ride home.

As I stood outside, waiting in the cold, this 40ish Jewish man with a thick New York Yiddisher accent approached me. "Do you know the way to the Smithsonian?"

"End of the block make a right, can't miss it."

"Do you want to take classes?" he asked me.

"I don't understand."

"Well it's important that the children have only one religion, and better that it be your religion," his finger points at me, "than her religion," he points

at Sam as she approaches. (She's Korean-American)
I guess he saw us together in the museum and cared
enough to follow me out into the cold to give me
this advice. I'm disgusted/repulsed/shell-shocked
beyond words and start to walk away, but hear him
mutter, "So you're dating a shiksa."

And I couldn't even begin to explain what had
happened to Sam and Maureen. And once again I
played the role of an adult wearing a yellow feather
covered costume talking about some hairy invisible
elephant. But it really all did happen. I swear.

Despite all that, we had a good visit. Maureen
sends her love.

Thanks for listening.

Love,
Elliot

P. S. If anyone ever tells you that high school is
the best four years of your life, don't get suicidal.
Hang in there, it gets better. High school sucks,
everything afterward is definitely better, previous
two stories to the contrary. I love my job, and I'm
usually having a really good time. If you need any
humentashen ammo...

No one signed up. Sucks that I'm madder at the
politicos, who I feel like should walk the walk, than
at the fashion punks who I knew would do nothing.
Probably for the better. Imagine punks tutoring.
"We can't read this book to children. It shows the
garbage men smiling, which is part of the way the
system reinforces class roles."

Accessory after the fact. I feel like I should write
in code, so that this evidence cannot be used

against me. Guy I know at work, D.J. , came in and told Evan about killing these two "small time thugs." Don't think that he'll get caught.

Considered dropping a dime, but mostly just wish I didn't know. Which is kind of a fucked-up, hear no evil attitude, but it makes me nauseous and sad.

Violence walks through this city like a dumb, dangerous caterpillar. Like one of those caterpillars with spikes that sting. And the powerful hire police to keep the caterpillar corralled into an area far away from them, not caring enough to actually try to figure out what's up, wherefore and whyfore comes this beast. No discussion or caring (or worse, discussion without caring) about those who live daily where the police encourage the caterpillar to stay. And the police do their job, more or less, and on the rare occasions that the beast "gets loose," it's usually slow and awkward and tremendously outgunned... And we, "we" make made-for-tv movies and get close-up looks at those powerful spikes.

And then punks and do-gooders live at the edges of this violence, for the more raw and real life. Showing where our "real" sympathies lie. And tell ourselves how we're not a part of that other world. "I mean, I don't even pay taxes, so, you know, they aren't my police force."

———

Date? with Jenny. Not very fun, not very exciting. Think that I could kiss her if I wanted to, which I don't think that I do. The excitement, I guess, is that I could.

Ah, the conquest theme. Christa would be so pleased.

———

Not a bad day after all. So we'll tour. Pretty stoked to leave town, get the hell away from all of these people. So many years watching people get on stage and do it, can't wait to see what it's like. If every half-talented musician can get on stage, at least I can get up there and not be stupid, or say something. I wonder if we can stay with Super Vixen in Seattle. Ha.

I wonder if T or J know anyone with a video camera. That they want us to take all over in a van and get food and our feet on.

Reread tonight *Soul on Ice*. Sickly, insanely, pathetically wished that I had been given fewer freedoms, so that I could fight the good fight. The "genuine"/"authentic" liberation struggles aren't mine, and I sometimes wish for my own Warsaw Ghetto Uprising. All this fucked up shit floating around in my brain, being attacked with great cunning/ acumen and the glorious end result is that the language that I use is slightly more inclusive.

I see a lot of white kids my age "acting black," and looking silly, though it's easy to see the attraction. The story of the underdog, playing against a stacked deck, against a system loaded with guns and laws and couched in hypocritical, noble-sounding terms- well you'd be an idiot and asshole not to find the story compelling, not to see some of the truest minutes of beauty in the victories, not to admire anyone doing their part in the struggle.

And the white kids are born (I am born) into privilege (so are a lot of black kids privileged, in a lot of ways, but I haven't walked any miles in those shoes, and I am trying to judge). And the struggle to use that privilege against the system isn't full of flashy passion, but just the slow burning sensation of doing something to make the world a little better than you found it.

Once upon a time, not so long ago, in a village very close by, there lived a little girl. She was born into a family that seemed very happy. They had a big house, and plenty of food to eat. The family was waiting, though. A long time ago, there had been a man who had claimed that he was going to make everything better in the world. Then the man had gone away, promising to come back and save the world from all of its problems. There were lots of people who were waiting for him to come back. And during this recess, during this in-between period, many of these people had decided whose problems that the man would fix, and to whom he would give worse problems. These people were making lists of those people who had been bad, and they stood ready to tell the teacher. Those that had been bad were going to have to spend forever holding up heavy textbooks on outstretched arms. Those that had been good were going to game-time and ice cream. Forever.

The little girl's parents had decided that people who had sex for reasons other than children were going to have to hold textbooks. Especially if it was with people of the same gender. They told themselves that they were blessed to have been given the criteria for judgment. So blessed. They collected money to send people all over the world to tell everyone. So that everyone would be warned that they will have to hold heavy textbooks. And who would chose heavy textbooks when they could get game-time and ice cream?

Every Wednesday and Sunday the family worked extra hard, and talked about exactly what the criteria were. And as she grew, she learned about how many things could stop her from getting the ice cream that she had been offered. Drinking, smoking, drugs, sex, bad words- all of them could make you lose game-time, forever.

When she was fourteen she got to work with the older kids to spread the criteria that the man was going to use. This made Christa very happy, because she believed and loved the truths that she had been taught. But the strange thing was that these kids spent a lot of time doing the things that might make them lose ice cream. But only when none of the adults were watching. Sometimes when they would get caught they would say that bad men made them do it. Sometimes they would say that they were sorry and cry and accept the criteria again. Christa, the now not-so-little girl, was very sad that the other children in her group might lose ice cream. She had a friend, Beth, who also believed, without time-outs, the truth of the word. And all through tenth and eleventh grade they did everything together. They prayed, studied, volunteered at the church, wrote letters to prisoners to spread the word. The summer before senior year, they went together to Church Retreat in the mountains in Virginia. On the first night, all the presidents of the youth group made speeches of invocation, and the way that Robert spoke made Beth and Christa's hearts leap. "It says very clearly, 'I set before ye this day a blessing and a curse.' And then goes on to tell us how to choose the blessing and therefore eternal life. But think about it, y'all. There are so many people who've never had the chance to be told the good news. Who've never had the chance to choose the blessing. And that breaks my heart."

When he was done speaking, Robert came over and sat down next to Beth. She told him how much she enjoyed his speech, how blessed they all were to hear his words. Beth and Robert took a long walk that night, and at lights out, Beth told Christa that she liked Robert a lot. "He's so passionate about our Lord. He has so many good ideas about how to spread the word." The next night they again took a long walk, and Beth told Christa that she thought that she might want to marry Robert, that she had always wanted to be a preacher's wife. Then on the third night, after their walk, Beth could only cry, nodding answers to Christa's questions. Robert had stolen the most precious gift that a girl can give to her husband. And three other girls in the cabin told similar stories about boys in the youth group. Christa couldn't be in the youth group any more.

Her parents didn't want a daughter who did not love the Lord. Even if she said that she did, she didn't want to go to youth group any more, and they wanted the kind of daughter who was grateful for the word and felt honored to work to spread the word. Two choices: youth group or out of the house.

Out. She wanted out of the house. She couldn't go back to church, didn't want to stay in her parents' house. A few of her friends that had also left the youth group had a house. And they observed most of the criteria, they didn't drink, do drugs, smoke, have sex, or eat meat. And it seemed right, because they really did none of these things. They didn't promise one day and then drink the next. Or have sex when the girl didn't want to.

And so she left home and moved into the house, with her parents in shellshock that their only daughter was choosing holding textbooks over game-time and ice-cream. One of the women in the new house was a stripper, which even if it wasn't the sex that was forbidden, was part of the sexual world. In her new house she and her new friends talked a lot about How Fucked Up the World Is. Together they decided that they had been told many lies about the criteria, and maybe the whole story had been a lie. No game-time forever. Christa started to swear, and sometimes she would drink alcohol. Also she began to wear clothes that her parents and church said were evil. She went around wearing shirts with pictures of girls kissing girls, "Read My Lips."

But in real life at the end of her lips was no one. No girls, no boys, no one. She and her friends talked about the way that the Death Culture had programmed them to like boys or girls that looked certain ways, but they were going to fight back.

When a certain Jewish boy with a big nose and bad posture came into her life, Christa saw an excellent opportunity to apply theory to real life. She remembered that the original man in her life, the one that she had been waiting for all of these years, was a Jewish boy who yielded not to temptation. She had high hopes for the experience.

He was proof of her success in liberating her desires from the ones that the Death Culture had tried to force upon her. She found that she liked to have someone to call and cry with, and that it was nice to occasionally find someone at the end of her lips.

This Jewish boy, however, had not struggled enough against the desires instilled in him by the Death Culture. She tried to lead him away from temptation, but he still thought that temptation could be satisfied, did not know that the only true satisfaction came with the death of desire.

Again and again she tried to show him the error of his ways, tried to explain how he ruined it for both of them by not trying to resist his desires. He doesn't want to save himself, and she can't paddle to safety with him holding onto her. So they part ways as she swims toward land, away from the Sea of Death Culture.

Bye-bye.

Sam was supposed to go shopping with the ladies next door, and they didn't answer the door. She saw them through the window earlier, so she went around back to see if they were on the back porch. She came around the corner, saw them duck, and was like, "Hey guys, are we going shopping?" and they popped up and got ready to go. She asked them why they were hiding and they tried to deny that they had been. They tried to deny that they had ducked down after she saw them.

Sam said, "Hey, if you guys don't want to go shopping, fine."

I guess that was just too real for them. They got all defensive and tried to play it off, but she just came home and cried. I wonder if it's about her living with me, a known patronizer of the King's Castle. If so, I'm sorry, but our next door neighbors should be able to forgive Sam my sins, or at least be honest.

Hiding on the back porch.

Usually I think DC punk rock is like high school. Today seemed more like fourth grade.

CRUZAPALOOZA '95

Henry Rollins smokes a cigar as he rakes in his chips at the Malcolm X Beat The Man Black Jack Table.

Only last year, the Tibetan people were suffering horribly at the hands of the genocidal Chinese government, and now, thanks to Mike D, Ad Rock and MCA, the room is full of Tibetan monks pulling the

levers of the Che Guevara Rage Against the Slot
Machines and the Crazy Horse One Armed Bandits.
Converted from an oil tanker, with 137 channels
of cable, and permanent uplinks to the coolest, most
alternative sites on the world-wide web.
All of the slots are solar powerec and recycled
from pinball machines, so it's all super-eco.
Man, we are so much radder than Boatstock III
or the 2 Live Cruiseliner. As long as I can get my
free Che tat for playing third stage. Viva la
revolucion!

> When I look around I see the chickens
>   are coming home to roost
> But we can use our zines as umbrellas
>   and not get hit by the chicken poop
> In thirty years the president of the
>   United States will have a tattoo
> A real cool one, REVOLUTION in red,
>   white, and blue.

There's a new program, latest and greatest grant.
It's about "test-readiness," to "counteract the cul-
tural biases of standardized testing." It involves
using our tutors to teach how to take multiple-
choice tests. It looks like this: "Let's study vocabu-
lary now. Alright, so which one of these words
means deserving... Good try, but actually, 'merits'
means deserving. Say that back to me, 'deserving
means merits'... Good job, now let's look at number
two."
So many ideas have been so badly played out. So
many bad, ineffective, half-heartedly, half-fundedly
flung... Good ideas end up better funded in other
neighborhoods, bad ideas, well at least they'll know
not to do that with their own children.
White people have little to glamorously "give."

Already taken and stolen and starred in too much. Sometimes a little hard not to want to be the star of the show. Ridiculous feelings of wanting acknowledgment for not being a racist, a feeling that at best is unproductive and at worst part of a racist mentality. But once I figured all this out I would be full of shit if I didn't do what I feel to be right. Still, sometimes I want to lead the revolution and get all of the revolutionary chicks.

All this theory for the simple idea of looking at children and wanting things to be right and pretty and not hurtful to them.

Eugene-maybe. Call again to confirm Bozeman, Rapid City, and Portland. I love the dialer. God, I love the dialer. How can people afford to make all the calls you need to set up a tour without one?

Stuffed records and then stuffed records and then we, um, stuffed records. Cool to hear and look at your own record, but a thousand record covers, lyric sheets and records... it's a little much to look at a thousand all at once.

Brian's stoked because the Inter Galactic Chaos Conspiracy sold out in a month and got picked up for distro by Cargo. Which he says, "greases the wheels," for the Pessimist Club 10 inch. He's gone ahead and ordered a second thousand. Hope he doesn't lose a lot of money on us. We might actually make back what we spent on recording.

Alright, so um, it's clearly time for some <u>Mindcleaner</u>. The stench of rotting garbage in my brain, well, it's making it hard to live with me. The neighbors are getting some restraining orders. Housemates are issuing ultimatums....

I play in a band. I was getting[1] dressed before our show the other day, and I was hit with an unfortunate dilemma. My usual policy for shows is that I wear whatever I had been wearing the day before. But yesterday's clothes stank, which[2] left me deciding. I looked through my wardrobe, considering... no, too fashionable, nope, too grunge, no, too crusty. It's a shitty feeling, catching myself thinking about fashion and looking cool. I try hard to avoid thought about fashion, wearing mostly hand me-downs, but even among the[3] hand-me-downs I have favorites, and it's based on how good I think I look in the clothes. Sometimes I get pissed about what a uniform alterna clothes have become, but sometimes I wish that it[4] actually was a standard issue uniform, so I would think less about my and everyone else's fashion. Being cool is a lame endeavor, but it's everywhere to the point of anti-cool being it's own cool competition.

It happens like this: I catch myself rehearsing introductions to songs in my head, trying to[5] make them funny or witty or pretty or

---

[1] Kurt Vonnegut's introduction to *Bluebeard*, "Tremendous concentrations of paper wealth have made it possible for a few persons or institutions to endow certain sorts of human playfulness with inappropriate and hence distressing seriousness. I think not only of the mudpies of art, but of children's games as well- running jumping, catching, throwing. Or dancing. Or singing songs." Or punk rock. Or making little books.

[2] *Dogfight*. River Phoenix's and Lily Taylor's best movie ever.

[3] *Tampopo*, The structure. Also the only sexy sex I've ever seen on film.

[4] The Coup "Kill My Landlord"

[5] Receiving mail

interesting. I guess that's good; who wants to be bored by[6] the person on stage. But then I start thinking about talking about politics (which is what's on my mind a lot) and I find myself getting grossed out. I'm disgusted that it's "cool" to talk about Mumia Abu Jamal while on stage. It's gross that I'll be sexier if I talk about oppression (mostly other people's). But it's also gross to be in[7] the spotlight and say nothing about all the bullshit that's going on in this world. And it's lame to feel like you never have the right to be in the spotlight.

This MC mostly was done long ago, but me and[8] my backsliding, devil-worshipping ways, postponed and postponed, until judgment day arrived, and me so stuffed with shit that my colonologist charged me for two visits. At least he salvaged some Mindcleaner.

So enclosed herein please find the following 1) Christa's farewell column 2) Prisons, an infomercial 3) DC Fashion, a doctoral thesis by Kate Ph.D. 4) This week's haftorah portion, in which Elliot the Bar Mitzvahed visits Atlantic City. 5) The usual reviews and[9] other boring punk shit.

Thanks to everyone who's written to me... If you ever want to write anything about something in the zine feel free, I might print it. Otherwise, keep[10] sending me the marriage proposals and major publishing contracts, but I'll keep turning them down...

---

[6] Having a job that doesn't suck

[7] Ward Churchill and Jim Vanderwall

[8] Los Crudos

[9] Diggable Planets' "Blowout Comb." Wins the liner notes of the year award.

[10] Sherman Alexie's *Lone Ranger and Tonto Fist Fight in Heaven*. Best book my parents have ever given me.

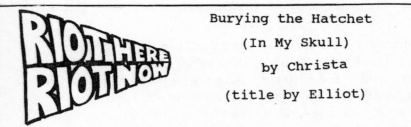

Burying the Hatchet

(In My Skull)

by Christa

(title by Elliot)

So this column is about how Elliot, the cool
punk kid who puts out this zine, manipulated me
in really uncool ways when we were involved. Not
that he manipulated me, because I am too smart to
be manipulated by someone else, but that I let
myself be manipulated in the situation. And that
kind of manipulation, and the ways that we dont
challenge it are part of the culture of sexual
violence against women. Which leaves me feeling
like shit.

And that's why we can't be friends.

And right now, I'm getting angry that he's going
to be seen as sensitive or cool for printing
such a hostile column.. So don't print it. But
you're a weak suck if you do print it and a weak
suck if you don't. Mostly you're lame and I
hate you.

What happened might be written off as chump
change, but there are no small points..
Everything is

What happened might be written off as chump
change, but there are no small points.
Everything, everything is connected. The way
that my body could be"conquered terrain" to you
after we sleep together and the way that I
always worry about this, even when you were
enjoying yourself. The language that we use
to describe how this happens, active and passive
verbs, it all has to do with how you treated me,
and how I will never forget any of this..
NEVER. Fucker.. Fucked her. Got fucked.
Had her. Been had.

And many of you are now piqued, curious, excited.
But I'm not going to paint you a picture vivid
enough to get your rocks off to. Fuck you.

And now I'm getting madder and madder about
how I'm a contributor to this. And how much
xw rawer and more intense I'm making this zine.
How Elliot wrenches from me, and then somehow
I'm trained to still give parts, hurting parts
of me.

I AM THE SOUL OF THIS ZINE, BUT I REFUSE TO
GIVE ANY MORE PARTS OF ME TO ELLIOT, SO HE CAN
BE COOL FOR ORGANIZING SOMETHING COOL- BULLSHIT!
THIS ZINE IS NOT COOL.

And I am not a man-hater, but I hate Elliot.
And I hate you, Mr. reader. I hate you for
reading this and thinking that I am crazy.
I AM a man-hater. I cannot write for men's
zines anymore. Men have controlled
my creativity, I have given too
much to men already. I am not
writing so that men can read this,
because they can never understand
what I'm talking about anyway
and will only see what they want
to see in my words anyway.

I REFUSE TO HAVE MY WORDS
BE PART OF ANY MALE'S
PUBLICATION.

-Christa

COME HERE LITTLE GIRL AND SIT ON GRANPA'S LAP
D.C. FASHION   by KATE

Why do they call it second hand clothing
when the first person to own it (odds are) had
two hands.... It should be called third and
fourth hand clothing. But that's neither here
nor there... Today's first order of business, to
detail for you Mr. and Ms. Reader, the fashion
event of the season, last week's Celebrity
Ghouls event at Chateau of Foreign Affairs. The
place to see and be seen in the D. C. scene.

The cause for the evenings celebrity
gathering: a fashion show. All of our favorite
scenesters were there to see the lovely and thin
women of the Mt. Pleasant rock crowd parade down
the runway in their beautiful vintage 60's and
70's apparel which threw their images straight
back to the days of grade school and lunchboxes.

But the sense of style was not confined to
the runway. Anthony of Marchenko made the scene
in a stunning brown cardigan, reminiscent of the
50's. He was overheard whispering to an unknown
man in a stunning brown cardigan(reminiscent of
the 50's): "I'm really different because I like
old music, you've probably never heard of it,
it's called jazz." The evening's sveltest host,
Aaron Pavapolous, was sporting a gorgeous green
cardigan, straight out of the 50's accessorized
by a wallet chain which added a sense of
rebelliousness to the ensemble. He was
overheard chatting with Evan Marks of Truman,
fully decked out in tight slacks, wallet chain
and deep blue cardigan. Tres 1953, Evan! The
conversation? "Personally, I go for older cars,
you know like Ford Fairlanes." "Really? That's
so bizarre, because I love to listen to jazz
while I work on my Dodge Dart."

Back on the runway, Christine Allen of
Toronado 75 could be seen in a splendid halter
top/ short shorts ensemble circa 1978.
Accessorized gorgeously with a Three's Company
lunchbox. Grace, of Monsoon fame, made the
scene in a gorgeous soccer shirt/tight pants
combination, with pigtails flying. Wow, she
knows how to use those plastic barrettes that

some of us remember so well from the 70's.
Backstage, the uncommon sounds of be-bop era
"jazz" could be heard on the hi-fi while the
girls discussed Amy Summers' purchase of a
gorgeous '65 Ford Fairlane. The finale of the
fashion show came when Johnny Connor, in a
stunning brown cardigan and tight polyester
slacks, escorted a pink mini skirt, Jordache t-
shirt and bouncing blonde pigtails adorned
Christina Williams to the end of the runway.

Fantasy dialogue: "Come here little girl,
sit on Grandpa's lap. We can talk about jazz or
whatever else comes up."

The Paparazzi was on hand, snapping photos
with their vintage flashbulb cameras and
capturing the whole event in stunning super-8.

Disclaimer: Things might be this bizarre in
other cities as well, but since I couldn't
afford to buy a Dodge Dart or Ford Fairlane, I
couldn't leave D.C. to check out the scene in
other towns.

Elliot Goes To College:
AKA The stupidest things heard this week.

with all the rights, honors, and privileges appertaining thereto.

So I've been taking a class at the University of Maryland in College Park, MD. "Race Relations in the United States," with Carlos Aguila. First structured class that I've taken since graduating high school two years ago. It's pretty mediocre. Definitely adds fuel to the blazing belief that I'm getting a better education outside of the institution than I would within.

The course goes like this. The professor assigns some reading (frequently from the book, <u>Anglos and Tejanos and Beef</u>, which he wrote, that we have to purchase from him at $20 per paperback). Then we come to class. He opens by asking if we have any questions about the text. One of the kiss ass sorority grrrrrls asks if he could explain the second chapter. The professor opens the book and reads, verbatim, with no explanations for 45 minutes. Then he talks about upcoming tests or papers. Then we go home.

The class is biggish, about 80 students. At least half are Jewish. Initially I was mortified, afraid that all the Jews would be total sixties connected (the ones who don't sport frat or sorority letters usually wear Grateful Dead Gear) I was afraid they'd be talking about how unracist Jews are due to our history of oppression and their ever so liberal work in helping to found the NAACP. I still feel profoundly embarrassed, but it's not because they're trying so hard to be unracist...

In a nod to the idea that students learn much from each

other, the prof decided that we were to present five minute summations of our papers. During one class he inquired as to the subjects of our projects. Lots of papers about discrimination in the workplace. The woman in front of me answers, "Well I was going to do my paper on Black-Jewish relations," (my nightmare come true.) "But," she continues, "I couldn't find any information." I'm incredulous, as a full 9 tenths of the books published yearly seem to be some Jewish man's claim to be a soul brother. She goes on, "So then I decided to do my presentation on race and rape," (and I'm thinking, cool, she's going to talk about the disparities between sentencing with the rapist and survivors' races taken into account) "like, you know, how it used to be mostly white men doing the raping and now it's mostly black men."

I am not even kidding, this woman really said that. IN A RACE RELATIONS CLASS. In 1993. And everyone (me included) said nothing. So I had to quickly pick my jaw off the floor to say: "Um, my paper is on race and the prison system."

It's pretty important to me to not judge someone until I've walked a mile in their shoes, and the thing is I feel like I've walked plenty of miles in these peoples' shoes. So, let me try to explain why they make me so damn mad:

I feel like most of the other Jews in my class, like me, have access to a lot of money and support to do a lot of things to work against racism and to reject some of the benefits that our racist society offers them. Beyond that, these are people who are actively Jewish, involved in Jewish Fraternities and Sororities, and part of Judaism is the mandate that it is every human's job to make the world a better place. And most seem severely blinded to the ways that they perpetuate/perpetrate... Urrrgh.

IN AMERICA,
MOST RAPISTS ARE WHITE.

PRISONS IN AMERICA

I started thinking a lot about prisons when I put out the first issues of mindcleaner and started getting mail from prisoners all over the country. I wanted to know more about the prison system in America and maybe say something to the folks in my Race Relations class, especially to those who believe things like that "most rapists are black" shit. The following article is a summary of the information that was in my paper, which I presented to the class. The whole paper is about 15 pages, and I'll make you a copy if you send me stamps.

To really understand the functions of prisons in our society, it's important to look at the history of American Prisons and how they have related to American society as a whole. I'm not gonna quote entire chapters of history texts, but I think that we can agree that the land that our country sits upon was stolen from people who we (represented by our government) continue to break treaties with and screw over in immoral and illegal ways. The US rose to world prominence with the "help" of slave labor. For over 200 years, our country, our government, our forefathers took part in kidnapping humans in Africa and selling them into slavery and torture. Our Supreme Court, our congress, our presidents discussed in broad daylight, on paper, how to buy, sell, and tax human chattel. This is part of our legacy as Americans: Genocide and Slavery. It was little more than 100 years ago that slavery was abolished, and it is impossible to know the extent of the impact that slavery and subsequent discrimination, often supported and enforced by law, has had on conditions today. It is our legacy to choose or refuse, the genocide and slavery of yesterday is not our fault, but what still goes on today that we choose to do nothing about will be our fault tomorrow.

By the year 2000 over half of all African American men will have spent time in prison. Latinos are imprisoned at a rate which is double their proportion in US society as a whole. Two out of every seven Native American men have been imprisoned in their lifetimes. 54% of women in prison are women of color.

The high percentages of people of color in prison show the biases of the those who make and enforce the laws of the country. The history of inequality and discrimination show up both in the economic divisions in this country as well as in the actual laws of the land. While individuals often "successfully" swim against the tide of American society, the society reflects the unjust laws and history.

Sentences are generally harsher for people of color. Judges and juries impose the death penalty disproportionately on people of color. Even though African Americans are murdered at a higher rate than whites, ninety percent of all death sentences are "justice" in cases where a white person died.

Many women convicted of violent crimes were defending themselves or their children from abuse. On average, prison terms are twice as long for women who kill their husbands as for men who kill their wives.

Within the next hour, three people in the US will have died as a result of violent crime. In the same time period, four people will die as a result of unhealthy or unsafe conditions in the workplace. More often than not what we consider to be crimes are acts perpetrated by the poor, not acts perpetrated by the wealthy, such as allowing lax safety standards in the work place or on products available to the public. This also defines who we consider a criminal. Or, as a man incarcerated in Texas wrote to me, "The crimes that poor people commit cause them to end up in prison, and the crimes that rich people commit cause them to make more money."

Most women in prison have been incarcerated for economic crimes. 80% of incarcerated women report incomes of less than $2,000 in the year before their arrests.

Healthcare in prisons is inadequate. Lack of staff and ancient equipment often compound the problems of sick inmates. Prisoners with AIDS are often denied basic healthcare, resulting in half the expected life span for those diagnosed with AIDS who are in prison as for those who are not.

Prisons don't stop crime, they are an extension of a justice system which is biased against the poor, women, and people of color. The fact that the United States has a higher incarceration rate than any other country in the world does not reflect the criminal nature of our society, it illustrates the confused priorities of our government.

One of the most important factors in the continuation of oppressive prison conditions is the fact that the vast majority of the public is greatly uninformed as to how the criminal justice/prison system really works in and what roles it actually plays in society. We too often allow our opinions to be shaped by the mass media and the prison/legal system's propaganda.

90% of women in prison are single mothers and once they are incarcerated they often lose contact with their children. In the US the mothers of 167,000 children are incarcerated.

In the past 25 years, the portion of the US population in prison has increased 500%. Spending on the criminal justice system is skyrocketing. Big businesses, already owned by those in power receive our tax money to construct more prisons and then earn more of our money selling supplies, etc. to the jails. That means that issues concerning prisons are affecting greater and greater portions of the population, but only the interests of the wealthy are being served.

I guess that's the main parts of the paper. It's depressing/disgusting, what's going on. My main hope is that one day we can look back at the prison system/criminal justice system as a fucked-up part of our nation's history, something that we are embarrassed about, like slavery or Japanese internment camps. But that means we need to do things to end the system. Today.

BY THE YEAR 2000, 1 OUT OF EVERY 150 AMERICANS WILL BE IN PRISON.

WHAT WE CAN DO

1. Don't vote for "tough on crime" politicians. Politicians are always creating enemies. Commies "necessitated" more weapons, bigger and more powerful. Today's criminals "necessitate" bigger and badder jails. Less rehabilitation. Less rights for human beings caught up in the prison system.

2. Work with or join organizations that work on Human Rights in the American Criminal Justice System. American Friends Service Committee and Anarchist Black Cross are two such groups. Or start your own.

3. Recognize that not everyone in prison is a menace to society. Recognize that many of the greatest threats to the common good will never go to prison.

4. Realize and let others know that laws are made by humans, who make mistakes. The law of the land is not sacred, and is often immoral. It was recently legal to own, buy, and sell other human beings. It was recently illegal to purchase alcohol, illegal to touch the person you love in certain ways, illegal to vote if you were a woman or a person of color or without property.

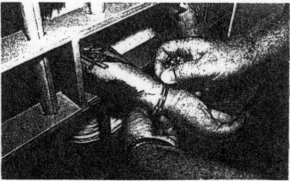

THE HEART OF BRIGHTNESS: ELLIOT THE BAR-MITZVAHED'S SOJOURN AMONG THE INFIDELS AND OTHERWISE STRANGERS TO THE GOSPEL OF THE CHURCH OF LATTER DAY OF PUNK ROCK

(I confess, I write about travel so that I can deduct it as a business expense.)

It was 11 o'clock on a Saturday night. We had exhausted our supply of kicks for the evening/week/year/lifetime. It was that suburban feeling of nothing to do in a small town, but we weren't in a small town. The perverse and altogether unpunk idea appeared in our minds like a light bulb in the dark night of our boredom: Atlantic City.

Within minutes, we were in the car, gambling money in hand, wearing our finest polyester leisure suits, looking like the big-time players that we are. We drove through glorious New Jersey under a blazing 3:00 am moon. We stopped at Walt Whitmanland on the Jersey Turnpike for pinball and coffee and to kow tow at the altar of the first of the revelatory acts of Deity of the Church of Latter Day Punk Rock (the Miracle of the Ride to Connecticut and the Deus ex machina as Mechanic)

And then we rolled in to the mother of all gaming towns. A place that gives genii like Donald Trump (what vision, to build a modern Taj Mahal) and Frank Sinatra the respect and veneration that they so richly deserve.

The early rounds went to The Man. Took me 3 hours to break even, playing the quarter slots. Tomothy, disappeared for two hours, and came back talking, "Forgive me dear, but I lost all our money," and when asked if he won or lost would feign sobbing. Kate lost $2.50 and quit. Colin, acting the part of country boy in the big city, through sheer dumb luck, couldn't lose a hand at the Black Jack Table and with grace and charm and a southern accent and huge tips to the cocktail waitress won $285. And paid for tolls and gas all the way home.

Arriving home, we devised several computer programs, did some Lexus Nexusing, and figured that, after tolls and gas money, we were some $20 poorer than when we left. Negative $20, and no miracles.

Well at this point, regular readers are probably wondering, "what's up?" The lesson of this week's portion is a subject of furious debate among the students of the gospel. Some Rabbis argue, passionately, vehemently, with little rivers of spittle threading through lip rings and down their wizened goatees, that when you forget the tenets of your faith, well, you can't expect fireworks, passionate sex, or any other miracles. This interpretation holds that the Goddess is an omnipotent, all-knowing, and exacting creator. The letter of the law is to be followed, and any interface with The Man is an abomination in Her eyes. And abominations are not rewarded with miracles.

Others, followers of Rabbi Godisgoodenstein, with equal passion and twinkle in their eyes, argue that the Goddess, by choosing to not perform a hail and pillar of salt miracle, wishes to do two things:
1) Test the faith of the flock, just because she doesn't reveal herself on every street corner does not mean that she is not there and powerful and 2) Demonstrate the more subtle miracles of every day life, i.e. the safe return of all sojourners, the moments of beauty and hilarity that were afforded us. It shouldn't take a fixed Chevette, a free tank of gas, or a talking bush to keep us eternally faithful.

And the skeptics, bah humbuggin like always, say, "When you go to a place with fewer punk rockers, fewer coincidences occur."

to:

Mindcleaner
PO Box 1666
Washington DC
20001

US Tour
June
&
July
1993

Chicago,

Pandering for other people's attention is one of the most loathable activities to catch oneself doing. Saying things that you don't really mean, or that you don't even know if you mean, just trying to be clever without thinking about substance or the corner that you might paint yourself into, or the foot that may soon be stuck in your mouth.

It takes months, years, a lifetime, to counteract the need for constant approval, constant attention. Re-evaluate every motivation for every action. Learn to be true to yourself to do what you want, because it makes you happy. Of course other people's happiness always factors into your own. You must find a balance, walk precariously, between truth and brown-nosing, honesty and niceness.

And when you do find that balance, that fulcrum of true-to-selfness, nothing is more annoying than people who haven't found it, and steal your spotlight and get all the chicks.

June 7

Dear Maureen,

Finally arrived at the publication headquarters of our favorite zine, *The Kate Moss Journal*, a spirited defense of thin women in general, and supermodels in particular. The author writes "Kate has endured much ridicule and scorn because of her looks, but the rejection of her body shape has proportionally increased the size of her soul. This kind of narrow interpretation of proper women's body shapes has left thin women on the sidelines for too long. This magazine celebrates what all other magazines denigrate- the thin woman." I don't think that he's joking.

Mostly he seems pretty nice, and he set up a show where we got paid and there was a crowd eager to see us. But it's hard to trust him much, and he's spent most of his time so far trying to get into Jordana's pants. Not to mention, everyone in his house is wearing Toronado 75 T shirts. Your description of their show in Oberlin was hilarious. How do such 2D caricatures walk and breathe? They came through every town that we've been in about two weeks before us, and I get the feeling that everyone is vaguely disappointed that we're not dressed more hip, that our women don't look more, well, more anorexic. It's like everything bad about the DC "scene" has polluted the entire country, and you can't find refuge, even if you flee to Fargo, North Dakota. Aaaagh. When, how did it come to this? The main selling points of the Toronado Blues Explosion (whoops, did I say that?), so far as I can tell, are that they sound exactly like John Spencer Blues Explosion (a good model to copy, if you're gonna copy), but you get to see them for less money, and get to look at two really thin women in tight shirts.

Even though I haven't fully escaped it, it's great to be out of DC for a while. It's pleasant to be around people who enjoy having fun, and seem sincere. I've forgotten what it's like to meet people at shows who have energy to do things that seem important in their community. The "scenes" in these towns seem like they're more about a bunch of freaks hanging out and having a good time. Not about fashion and getting your record out on the right label.

What's up with Atlanta? How's summer school teaching? Did these third graders flunk, or is this "enrichment"? Who do I have to blow to get a good review of our record in the pages of Maureen Hall Correspondence? Seriously, what did you think?

Yours for the empowerment of Kate Moss and oppressed skinny women everywhere, I am,

Elliot Rosenberg

P.S. We played on someone's front porch in Minneapolis. It rained and the cops came and we had fun.

Scene I

Three white, one Asian, calculatedly scruffy people in their late teens/early 20s inside a white 84 Econoline van. One man and one woman ride in front; one man, one woman sit on musical equipment in back. A wooden platform stretches across most of the back of the van, covered with blankets, zines and dairy-free candy bar wrappers. Music of the early Sonic Youth/ Pixies genre plays on the car stereo. Man in passenger seat is listening to a walkman, unconsciously tipping his 32 oz. cup of soda with his right foot so that it occasionally spills onto the van floor. Both passengers in the rear are reading zines.

Wide shot: A barn-like building somewhere in Montana. A wooden sign above double glass doors reads "The Filling Station: A Watering Hole". The gravel parking lot stretches from the front of the building around the left side and is full of pick-up trucks and Harleys. The van (with stickers on the back doors and bumpers i. e. "Avail" "Free Leonard Peltier" and "Corporate Rock Still Sucks") pulls into the parking lot.

Tight shot: Driver's side door, lower half. Door opens and a woman's shoes emerge. (Punk rock variety: worn, brown canvas with 1 and a half inch rubber soles.)

Camera follows shoes as they walk on dusty gravel to rear of van, joining three other pairs of shoes- Dr. Martens, Blue All-Stars, and Airwalks.

Docs kick at crumpled cigarette package in gravel as conversation proceeds:

"Yikes, Scooby."

"Maybe we could call from a rest stop and say that our van broke down and that we can't make it."

"It's not all-ages, we'll probably end up getting our asses kicked."

"Let's just check it out. Tomothy can always feign an asthma attack."

A few seconds of silence, a piece of gum is spit onto the ground, shoes begin to walk towards door.

"Seen *The Blues Brothers* lately?"

Scene II

A large, poorly lit tavern, dead animals and license plates adorn the walls. The sound of billiards and video games are faintly audible, occasional whoops or "aaawwwrrgh"s. The two men from the van and the woman driver are on stage with guitar, bass, and drums. Two people in baseball hats stand about 12 feet from the stage, other than them, the dance floor is empty. "Sweet Home Alabama" plays on the Juke box.

The guitarist, a lanky boy with messy, dyed hair (very photogenic, handsome, sexy, tries hard to conceal his good looks... where was I?) wearing a Nomeansno t-shirt and blue All-Stars says:

"We're ready to play, if y'all wanna turn down the juke box..."

There are faint mutterings of dissent from the darkness, but the music is eventually turned down.

Guitarist: "Don't worry, we play both kinds: country and western."

Drummer clicks a four count and band begins to play music that according to *Citypaper* sounds like: "Scrawl meets the Kinks on the wrong side of the tracks."

Band plays to little reaction. Pool games continue. Patrons at tables near stage watch like a television program that'll do until the next hour's good programming begins. Song finishes. Smattering of applause, mostly by woman seen earlier in van and twenty-something-ish promoter.

Guitarist: "Thanks. This next song is about Marion Penitentiary..."

Rough male voice from crowd: "Been there. Done that."

Guitarist (clearly rattled): "Um, really? How was it?"

Male voice: "That was a nasty place."

Guitarist: "That's what I hear, so this next song is for you... We have lyric sheets on the table next to the sound board..."

Band plays song. Woman from van passes out lyric sheets. Bar sounds are muted on soundtrack, as song plays.

Lyrics: "Marion/ Is there for us all/ Lockdown/ Mind/ Body/ Soul"

At song's end a few hoots and more clapping (enough to intimate that maybe, just maybe, the city-slicker band is winning over...)

Guitarist: "So what did you think?"

Male voice: "That's about what it was like."
Scene III

Band onstage, packing equipment. White male in early thirties, sandy mustache of the CHIPS variety, with the voice that earlier shouted, "Been there. Done that." speaks with the guitarist about prisons in the U. S.

Scene IV

Inside van: Bassist and Roadie argue in back seat. Drummer (who has been trying to read zine by dashboard lights) eventually joins argument. Topics ranging from loading equipment to status of upcoming shows to actual text of Henry Rollins' left bicep tattoo.

Camera rotates and tightens on Guitarist (driving). Nonverbally, through a complex series of mouth and eyebrow movements, he demonstrates that he is having an epiphonic moment. We can almost watch the cogs of his brain turning, cartoon style, as he moves his lips and eyebrows. These are his thoughts: "Take It Easy" playing on the joke box... a bunch of kids in second-hand clothing singing about the government... a bunch of zines and records?

He's smart, huh?

Luminaries say yes. Tim says he never offered a show. Now we've promised another band a gig in DC and we can't even get one. Looks like it'll be nice show in our living room.
Tour van conspiracy theories: "Why Tim Won't Give Us A Show"
1. We suck. (Probably not the reason, most bands

who play El Pollo suck.)

2. The Boycott of Elliot begins- Tina works at King's Castle, Tim goes out with her, knows about my tendency to exploit women. Or one of us wore the wrong brand of shoes to a show or was seen eating the wrong food somewhere. Either way, we need to be taught a lesson that only being denied a show at El Pollo can teach us.

3. Oh yeah, we told Tri-State Transmitter that it's hard to get shows with him, another lesson we need to be taught.

4. Tim is overwhelmed by feelings of penis envy that arise when he sees Jordana, who reminds him of his mother.

June 16

Maureen,

Being on tour is almost too cliché to write about. When the drummer from Aerosmith showed up backstage at the Roxie to see if I wanted to do some lines, I knew that it couldn't go on like this....

For reals, though, all the things I feel and do seem like I learned them by watching rockumentaries about touring bands. All emotions- roadweariness, excitement, soul searching, loneliness, bad shows, drinking, playing pool, writing letters to ex girlfriends. All super clichés. I can't get over the feeling that I'm playing a part.

I feel like I need to be a different person to be happy doing this. I get tired of my role: too earnest, too serious, too much the one who fixates on how ridiculous rock'n'roll is.

I've been feeling like a caricature all day long for two weeks. I can't imagine how people could do this all the time. Maybe it's because we don't really expect to become famous, we're just out to have fun and increase awareness about things that we care about, but it's all taking place in a system set up for people who want to become famous.

But mostly tour is really fun and self absorbed in some intoxicating ways. Playing music we write, getting interviewed, listening to recordings of ourselves, watching videos of the shows we played, giving out our address, selling records of music that we made. It's really easy to forget that you're not that special or cool because you can write a few songs... Everyone around you is acting like there's something cool about you, which is something we all, on some levels, want to believe. Easy to see where some people get a "soul-ly-er than thou" attitude.

I've had a lot of time to read and write a lot of letters, when I'm not driving or charting our route. In South Dakota, we drove past hundreds of people on motorcycles heading to the Harley convention in Sturgis. The band that we played with there had a guy dressed up like a giant robot and they had a song where they did a bunch of Kung Fu fighting against the robot. In California we played a huge show at a club run totally by volunteers, mostly kids. Just seeing a lot of different places where the punk scene is really important to the kids involved has been cool.

I've forgotten what it's like to be in a place that still needs to be torn apart more than it needs to be put back together. (Does that make sense?) Acting crazy and having badly dyed hair and being happy and smart shows kids and adults that there are lives to be lived outside of either the Baptist or Episcopalian church... Like this: in suburbia the problem is that everything is so structured as to be lifeless and soul-killing, whereas in DC so much shit is entirely without structure that no one knows what the fuck is going on, to the point of being unable to trust anyone else.

Are travel letters always so filled with brooding analysis of society?

Yours in fond remembrance of more whimsical letters, I am I be I am,

Elliot Rosenberg

P.S. *Johnny Cash Live at San Quentin* has kept me sane (and driven my travel companions a little insane). There is this time where he plays the song, "San Quentin," that he wrote for the show: "San Quentin, I hate every inch of you/You cut me and scarred me through and through/ and I'll walk out a wiser weaker man/ Mr. Congressman, you can't understand."

It's the punkest minute ever recorded. The prisoners go as apeshit as they can with armed guards standing all around them, and make him play it two times in a row.

———

Bizarre. Bizarre. Bizarre. We got an indication of the craziness that is to come last night in New Orleans. We've been picked (selected?) by *Spin* as "keepers of the flame of DC punk."

A. ridiculous

B. gross and slimy

C. means crowds at our shows

About 100 kids in New Orleans. The big questions are: did *Spin* get promo stuff from Brian? Did Brian crop the photo or did *Spin*?

Making fun of *Spin* brought whoops and cheers. Same 10 songs, but now they're officially "good" so people can enjoy them more. Sold more records tonight than the first two weeks of tour. *Spin* says it's good, so...

The high school senior class is perforated beyond belief. *Farm Boys and Their Piercings* is RE/Search's next...

We got on stage and some creep whistled at Jordana. She said, "Thanks, I think that your mom is cute too." And the crowd laughed with Jordana at the asshole, and I felt a glimmer of hope. Played our regular show, with the exception that I introduced each song with, "This guitar line is about_____," making fun of something that I hated about living here. Topics ranged from stupid fights that everyone watches to couples walking around the mall with their hands in each others' back pockets. Each intro was met with roars of approval (even songs like "Marion" and "Stolen Land"). And it was bizarre to have the whole football team watching and cheering, but it was still pretty fun. Slam dancing started on about the third song. (Possible dialogue, "Hey, I saw people do this in that Nirvana video. Dude, it looks cool."). So they're at it, and it's annoying me and Jordana. We were in the middle of "Beat Schmeat, Drummer Schmummer" when I broke a string. As I tried to pull the string out of the way, I saw that the dancing had escalated into a fight. I stopped playing and so did Jordana and then Tomothy and all eyes turned to the fight. Jay, in his bleached hair and L7 shirt was on the bloody end of Patrick's punches. The football team arrived, etc. etc.

Local Boy Makes Good. Glad new attitudes came with the new fashion.

And that's the way that we end tour. Our last show will be in a laundry mat in Knoxville.

27 down, one to go, plus our living room.

Brian,

Saw the poster and promo shit that you've been sending out.

When we saw the picture in *Spin*, we figured that they had copied the back of the record cover and cropped the picture themselves. But after the same picture showed up on flyers in two cities, we figured something was up.

Did you cut off the top of Elliot's head and the side of Tomothy's face because you thought it looked more artistic, or were you just trying to put Jordana's tits in the very center of the photo, or is there a difference to you?

Getting the message from our housemates that you're pressing CDs was an extra-shitty touch. Thanks for not including us in any of this.

We put out a record with you because we thought that we could trust you. Actually, we thought you were our friend. We didn't want to make money, just to put out a nice record for people to enjoy. But now, with a little *Spin* assistance, you will be making plenty of money off of our record. Hope that makes you happy.

Obviously, our plans for recording and releasing a full length with 33rd Revolution are canceled.

Fuck you.

Sincerely,
Jordana, Tomothy, Elliot

My so-called home, Washington DC

While you're taking a shit, you don't always notice the stink, and it's not until you return to the john ten minutes later that you actually realize the magnitude of the smell. Five weeks of tour has truly cleansed the my nasal palette and I can truly say that it stinks to be back.

Homecoming royalty, time to face the tight pants mafia. Play a show in your living room because you're so revolutionary, not because you were a punk rock loser five weeks ago.

Unspoken deal: don't mention the shows that he wouldn't give us before we were famous, he pretends we've always been cool. What a big red-hair-dyed turd.

Tina: "I heard you were calling my band the Frank Gorman Blues Explosion," she says. Apparently the Toronado 75 has ears all over the country.

We looked at her for a minute. "No," Jordana said. "Sam might have said that though." Jordana, with a crisp pass of the buck.

"It really pisses me off when people say that. I mean first of all, we don't sound anything like the Blues Explosion, and second, why does everyone think that it's Frank's band? I mean, why not call it the Tina Cromwell Blues Explosion?"

"Uh... yeah."

"It really sucks the way women's contributions to punk rock are ignored. I think that our band puts out a real positive image for girls."

Jordana and I contemplate the positive messages behind some guy with a guitar jumping up and down with a waif-thin woman in a skin-tight outfit and six-inch heels on either side. Not to worry, though. Tina's ready to explain: "I think that girls come to see us, and it shows them that, like, even girls with larger bodies can totally get on stage and rock."

Like the frog in boiling water. I'm just noticing that the water around me has bubbles and steam and like all the best frogs are floating at the top. I wonder when things got this heated. And I've just enough left to try to leap out of the pot. I hope the frenchy chef is tending to the snails while I make my escape.

Thanks to: our families, MacGregor Mai, Hannah Tashjian, Kate Fodor, Becky Linn, Matt Clark, Jennie Papenthien, Darry Strickland, Josh MacPhee, Myla, Abby, Dara, Dahlia, Meghanne, Mark, Lizzie, Donna, Rebecca Parker, Susan, Chloe, Mary & Erika, Tim and Anamaria, Irene Chien, Don PunkLife, the Beehive, Ethan, Abe Isaacson, Angela, Damian, Kristen, Nathaniel, Meyer Elementary, Food Not Bombs, Anarchist Black Cross, Los Crudos, Zephyr copies, Epicenter, DC punk rock, 1727 Irving St. (and the next door neighbors), Rain Makes Applesauce and Eternalux and everyone who helped them on tour.

Also: Fugazi, KRS ONE, Bikini Kill, Chester Himes, John Edgar Wideman, Sherman Alexie, Billy Wimsatt, Dirty Three, Mr. Blanding's Dreamhouse, Johnboy, Spitboy, Jack O Fire, Jonathan Kozol, Big Sandy and the Flyrite Boys, Leonard Cohen, Johnny Cash, GooDie Mob, Emiliano Zapata, Efraín Calderón Lara (Charras), and the hundreds or thousands of people behind bars for doing the right thing. And anybody else who gives enough of a shit to try to make things better.

Jamie Schweser
used to live in Iowa City, where he ran a small media empire, fought the FCC, and rarely slept. He now lives in New Orleans, and still denies that he learned anything as an Oberlin College art major.

Abram Shalom Himelstein
lives in New Orleans. Some years he is a school teacher. He started New Mouth from the Dirty South, a publishing company.